South West Pacific
Motor Torpedo Boats

Follow my time in the PT Service
During World War 2

Book #1 of the South Pacific series

James Beck

Disclaimer:

This is a work of fiction. All characters and events and locations portrayed in this novel are either fictitious or used fictitiously and are products of the author's imagination.

Any resemblance to an actual person or place is not intentional but is used to allow for the flow of the story to progress as the actual war did. Any mistakes are mine and are not intended to try to change any actual historical account.

Dedication

This book is dedicated to my Father, C.E.C.S. John C. (Jack) Beck, USNR. He gave the Seabees his best in life for thirty-eight years, and he loved his Navy. It was his example that caused my brother and I to go into the Navy in the first place.

And to my three wonderful children, Cameron, Cassondra, and Chelsea.

Life would have been really boring without you along for the ride. Let your children have a vivid imagination, you never know where they will go in life with it. **JAB**

Construction Electrician Senior Chief,

C.E.C.S (Seabee) John (Jack) Beck-USNR

Table of Contents

Chapter 1 - From Notre Dame to the Navy

My brother Mike and I were attending classes at the University of Notre Dame and were getting ready to take our mid-term exams starting Monday, December 8th,1941. We were looking forward to the Christmas break that was to start after the exam week was over.

Mike was a senior that year and had a full-ride scholarship from the Rowing Team, and I was a junior with a 50% scholarship for track. Both of us were in the Naval Reserve program besides our heavy schedule of classes. That meant that we had to attend drills each week and learn about basic Navy stuff. We even got to take a month-long cruise on a WW1 Training Destroyer that was based on Lake Michigan in the summer of 1941.

We had to stand watches along with the regular sailors during the cruise and learn how things worked in our respective departments, they kept moving us around to give us extra training since they considered us "Boots." One of the neat things that summer, was that we got to visit different ports-of-call up and down Lake Michigan and Lake Superior's coastline like a real navy ship.

On Sunday, December 7th, we attended church service like normal at the University Cathedral even though we were not brought up as Catholic, but at Notre Dame, everyone was a "Catholic," so we went with a bunch of our friends to the 10a.m. mass. After lunch, we were going to join a few different study groups when we heard the news of the bombing of Pearl Harbor.

We had to look it up in a Geography book to find out exactly where Pearl Harbor was located to show our friends, Mike said that he had heard of it when we were on the Ship this last summer. I had no idea, but I was to learn about it really quick.

On Monday, the school postponed all the exams, so we listened to the radio and heard the President ask for a Declaration of War, everyone that remembers that day knows where they were when they listened to Roosevelt's speech that day, we were no different.

I told my brother that I wanted to go sign up right now, but he encouraged me to wait because things were going to be changing every day now that war had come to America.

He found out the next week from our Navy Captain in charge of our reserve detachment that the US Navy and Notre Dame University were going to offer any senior classmen the option to graduate early and take a commission as an Ensign in the Naval Reserve. We did not have to take any classes at the Naval Academy like in our original plans, we would get a Navy commission as an officer and get our orders right away.

Mike got his commission and left for a modified boot camp for officers on January 15, 1942. I had to stay behind till at least the end of the next semester before they would let me graduate early. I got my commission on June 5, 1942.

Mike and I wrote all the time, so I knew what to expect when I finally got to the Officer Boot Camp, He was right about a lot of things. His boot camp went for five months, but they had shortened it to 90 days by the time I went through it. That's why a fleet sailor would call us a "90-day wonder" behind our backs.

I went to a Navy base in Virginia for my Officer Boot Camp, we studied everything from naval history to gunnery and how to shoot the stars with a sextant to find out where you were when you were out to sea.

It was a long three months, but I made it through the classes with flying colors. I scored high enough on my final exams that I was able to pick my duty station from a list of forty-five that needed a new Ensign. I had picked a position as a Deputy Supply Clerk at a small airfield in Indiana.

I had sent a message home to let the family know that I would be coming home in a few weeks on leave before I had to report to my first duty station. We were told to report back to class at 16:00 for an important meeting so when I walked in, I saw where the duty assignments were all erased on the blackboard, and there were now the names of two ships. The USS Duncan and the USS James, I asked the school Commander what was up?

He said that the Naval Personnel had sent a message that they needed the next class of officers that were ready to graduate to be assigned to these two ships immediately. I told him that I was supposed to be going to a navy base in northern Indiana, he said that that assignment, would be offered to the next class, we were needed at our new duty station as soon as we could get there.

I was assigned to the Deck Department of a Destroyer named James, that was in "New Construction" at the New York Navy Yard. It was going to be Commissioned in about eighty days and was going to be sent to the Pacific Ocean, so we had a lot of work to do to get the ship and crew ready for sea.

This one day I was on the pier, supervising a working party loading stores up the gangway of the ship when I heard this beautiful, loud throaty sound coming from a boat down the river, whatever it was, it was coming upriver at a good clip. I had never seen a boat move so fast and handle so smooth in such a tight area. This was my introduction to a PT boat, and I was hooked from then on.

I had grown up around water all my life, Mike and I knew how to run boats like experts up and down the rivers and even on Lake Michigan, but I had never heard such power! It sounded like a caged animal that wanted to be let go and run at full speed.

I asked my Chief Boatswain Mate about the boat I had seen that day, and he laughed and said "Sir, those are called Motor Torpedo Boats," they call them a PT boat for Patrol torpedo-boat, and they are staffed by all volunteer crews just like a submarine. He said that they had just come out with them this last year.

Now I needed to find out about getting "off" this new destroyer and re-assigned to a PT boat. I called my brother who was on a one week leave at home and found out that he was just now assigned to "MTB Squadron-2" and was on his way to New Orleans to catch up with his new boat PT-66.

He told me that he had just finished his classes in Melville, R.I. and that they were short on officers so hurry my butt up, or I might miss the whole damn war. I went to see our Commanding Officer the next morning after morning colors and asked him to be relieved as the deck department boat ensign and to be transferred to Motor Torpedo Boats.

I had never heard an officer laugh so hard before, so I held my tongue until he was finished. He wanted to know why I wanted off his ship? So, I told him! He told me to get back to work and to stop dreaming about a plywood canoe, but I had caught the bug, and I could not get the thought out of my mind.

Talk about a long work day, in between all the training for the ship's company and the loading out of all the needed supplies and equipment we needed to load for the ship during the next week, it turned into a normal sixteen to twenty-hour workday, every day, with no time off for myself.

In the next week, I found out that the Officer-In-Charge of setting up the Melville R.I. PT-School was a Captain John Bulkeley, so I wrote him a quick letter explaining who I was, and who my brother was and why I wanted to join the PT boats.

A week later, I was called into my skipper's in-port office on the ship, and he was NOT a happy camper. He had my transfer papers in his hand, and he told me that I had exactly thirty minutes to clean out my locker and get off his ship.

He said that if he ever found out that I went over his head, he would make sure that I spent the rest of the war assigned to a tug-boat working out of Alaska. All I said was "Yes Sir! And Thank You, Sir!"

I made it to the Quarterdeck in a record time of fifteen minutes and got signed off by the Officer-Of-The-Deck. Then a quick 200-yard dash down the pier to catch a ride, I found some sailors loading torpedoes from a warehouse that were going to the torpedo school that the PT-School was using, so I bummed a ride with them.

They made room for me in the front of the truck, they told me they came down to the warehouse every two weeks to pick up another load of "fish" so it was no problem dropping me off. They were a nice bunch of kids, they were led by a crusty old chief that spent his time chewing on an old cigar and did not say very much to me. He might not have liked being in the middle seat. Melville, here I come.

#1- US Navy Photo- 1942 courtesy of Wikipedia

Chapter 2 - From Melville, R.I. to Panama

I made it to the front gate at the school that day and was told to report to the Administration Building for my assignment to a barracks. I was to spend the next three months living with eleven other guys in Barracks #5.

We were living in Quonset huts with wood floors and a wood stove at each end and one in the middle for heat in the winter. We had a standup locker for our hanging uniforms and a footlocker for everything else that we needed, the Navy figured if you needed anything, they would issue you one, if it was not issued, then you did not need one.

The school started out in March- 1942, with fifty-one officers and 177 enlisted sailor students that were all volunteers. Most of the original officers were hand-picked from the best of the "Ivy League" schools, Harvard and Yale provided a large number of the future PT-skippers. The first Cmdr. of the training school was William C. Specht, so the school took on the name, "Specht's Tech," he traveled to the different schools selecting whom he wanted for his program out of available seniors.

He liked the athletic type because they knew how to operate as a small team, and they were the leaders in school and could think on their feet.

In the beginning, at Melville, we had forty-seven Quonset huts in various stages of completion, they requested another fifty huts to help with the overcrowding.

Within a year or so, the school would acquire thirteen buildings for office space, thirty-four new classrooms, forty-two buildings for maintenance and almost two-hundred huts for living quarters. We were starting to look like a real school equipped to handle a normal load of 875 enlisted students and 90 student officers.

Until we got things down pat, we used the other training centers close to us, Naval Anti-Aircraft Training Center at Price's Neck, R.I.; Naval Torpedo School at Newport, R.I.; the rifle range at the Newport Naval Station and even the Packard Engine school in Detroit, MI. within a year, we would be doing most of our own training in-house.

We were given hands-on training by the engineers and builders at the ELCO Boat manufacturing plant in Bayonne, N.J. so that we became familiar with every inch of the boats that were consuming every minute of our lives.

My first skipper had called the PT boats a plywood canoe, but we watched them build this canoe, and I had nothing but praise for the boat builders.

Yes, they did use a lot of plywood, but the hull was not made of plywood, but two layers of mahogany planking laid over laminated wood frames for strength. A layer of airplane fabric that was impregnated with marine glue was ironed on between two layers of planking. The end result was a lightweight, extremely strong hull made to withstand heavy waves when we were out to sea.

They actually built the boats upside down at first to make it easier to build them.

#2 Elco Boat Co. 1942 Unknown author courtesy of Wikipedia

They tried out different engines but finally settled on three special made Packard twelve-cylinder marine engines rated at 1200 horsepower and running on 100-octane airplane gas. As the boats grew in size and weight more power was needed, and the engine size went up to 1350 and then to 1500 horsepower.

These engines were specially made for the Navy PT boats and were the most reliable items ever carried on a boat. The Packard Company recommended a major overhaul at 600 hours, but spare engines were not always available, especially in the war zones.

There were different types and sizes of boats built in the early part of the war by different boat companies trying to get the navy contract, from the fifty-eight-footer to the eighty-one-footer with the eighty-foot ELCO Boat was to become the standard for all future boats.

Each manufacturer laid out the inside a little differently, but they all carried enough fuel for

3000 gallons, of 100 octane fuel, and an engine room fitted out with three Packard 1500 hp engines (one engine was installed backward to make it fit between the other two engines). The exhaust was sent out the back of the boat and could be ran down into the water with a "muffler" attachment that would silence the sound at low speed, there were freshwater tanks, a chart-house for the radio, radar, map table, etc.

There was a wall for separation for the two officers, and the twelve to fourteen enlisted men in the berthing compartment and a small galley with an electric range and a small refrigerator ran by an auxiliary generator. There were two small "heads" provided one forward and one amid-ships, but the forward head was hardly ever used when we were out at sea due to the bouncing over the waves tended to make a mess that had to be cleaned up. We would use the headspace up forward for extra storage of food cans.

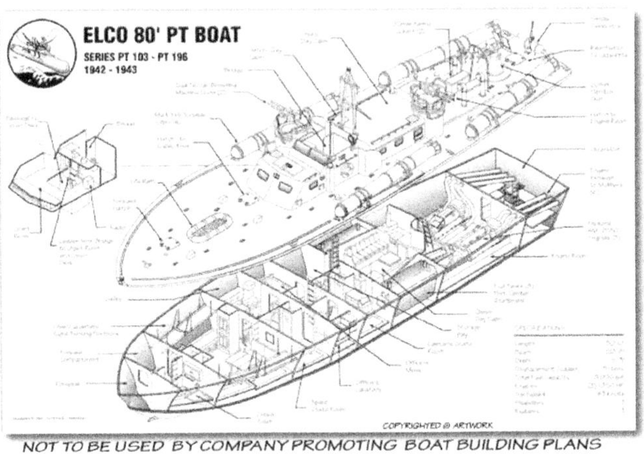

#3 Elco boat Diagram courtesy of Wikipedia

A normal complement of men on a boat was a Skipper, an X.O., a Chief, a Radioman, two

Enginemen, three Boatswain Mates and three Gunners Mates and two Torpedomen.

The first boats to go to war carried four twenty-one-inch torpedoes in heavy tubes that were shot out by a black powder charge and two pairs of twin-50 cal. machineguns in a turret on each side of the cockpit forward of the radio mast. There were also four Depth-Charges loaded on the stern, two per side in racks that would throw them out about fifty feet from the boat.

Some of the boats added a 50-cal. Machinegun forward for when they would board a small boat since the ones in the turrets had trouble aiming down into the water at close range and were really made for anti-aircraft use.

The black powder charge used to fire the torpedo tended to give away the location of the attacking PT boat when they fired their torpedoes at night and allowed the japs to focus in on the location with a searchlight, so the Navy developed a compressed air charge to send the torpedoes on their way. In the future, the school at Melville would develop a cradle that would roll the fish out and dump it into the water with the water igniting the motor.

#4 US Navy Photo -1944 Courtesy of Wikipedia

Later some boats added a 20 mm cannon for anti-aircraft/ small boat use.

Mike had been stuck in Panama "protecting" the locals from any chance of the jap menace, and he said that liberty was a blast in that part of the world. He had enough men and boats to work an eight-hour shift and then liberty for sixteen hours. But that came to a halt in July when they were notified to be ready for a move to the south pacific.

They brought three new boats to Panama to bring the total to fourteen boats, and they split up Squadron-2 to make a new Squadron-3 with eight boats, the remaining six boats were to stay in Panama for security duty.

The original Squadron-3 were the PT boats that were destroyed in the Philippines at the beginning of the war, and they were still carried on the books of The Naval Bureau of Supplies and Accounts. The individual boats were not commissioned as Naval craft, but the squadrons were commissioned as a Unit, and this was going to make a big Administration "SNAFU."

The new squadron-3 had wired a message for the request for its commissioning allotment of material and supplies which included: spare parts and engines, tools, charts, paint, raincoats, battle helmets, saltwater soap, generators and chain hoists and a thousand other small articles that they would need to run a squadron in a forward area.

Now came the typical snafu, the Navy Dept. in its infinite wisdom said they had already allocated this equipment to PT Squadron-3, in 1941. They still had the original squadron on their books from the Philippines, so they sent back a message that it was not their policy to issue the same equipment a second time.

The response at the squadron level was in typical Navy fashion and is NOT printable here today. It took a little arm twisting and a few long-distance cables to get it all sorted out, but they got the message to delete the original squadron and replace it with another squadron. It would have been easier if the powers that be in the Navy Dept. had moved the numbers up a bit and started with #5, since Squadron#4 was the training squadron based at Melville, R.I. for the duration of the war.

Mike and his boats made the trip all the way from Panama to Fiji then on to New Caledonia strapped on the top of two different Navy Oilers and were off-loaded at the piers, they were then towed to Espiritu Santo by two converted WW1 destroyers and released when they were around 300-miles from the Island of Tulagi.

Here they would travel under their own power during the night to their new base of operations and arrive at daybreak on October 12. By moving at night, they hoped to evade any enemy snoopers or bombers that might be up during the daytime.

The PT boats operated best after dark at this time in the war since radar was not in use yet so they would ride around at night looking for a tell-tail bow wave to show where a jap ship was coming from and where it was going to.

They also had info coming down the "Ladder" from Coast Watchers whenever they had some ships go past their hide-outs. These guys were some of the bravest "Australian Diggers" that had ever served "The Queen." Some of them were old "Constables" with their Native Deputies but as the war grew so did the need for new Coast Watchers.

The Coast Watching system was set up first in 1919 to help keep tabs on shipping traffic north of Australia, they used plantation owners and missionaries at first but by 1935 the Navy took over control before the war started, they started out at first using the local Constables that used to enforce the "Queens Law" in the area.

#5 Photo courtesy of Australian WW2 museum

Some of them were soldiers or were officers in the Royal Navy, and had fought the Germans in North Africa. They were brought home for one reason or another for injuries, and they would hide out in the bush on an enemy-held island with a couple of trusted natives on the islands and transmit a short radio-call when they saw any ships go by them.

They were constantly on the move because the japs were using radio-detection equipment to try to track them down, they would use the natives to carry the portable radio sets, and a hand-cranked generator to provide power to run the unit. They would limit their messages to thirty seconds at the longest and then sign off and dismantle the set and move on to another location on the island they were assigned to.

#6 photo courtesy of Australian WW2 museum

With Japan's entry into the war, this island screen became the front-line. The Coastwatcher's communicated by radio through existing radio stations or by tele-radios that had been loaned by the Naval Board. They were given some instruction and a code with which to make their reports on any hostile movements and to report any item of intelligence value.

It was a lonely and precarious existence, no family, no mail, they were alone with nature.

The coast-watcher would usually barter for food for their team from the local villages, and once in a while, you would find a native that had a run-in with the "Constable" at a previous time in their life. The native would give him up to the jap commander in the area, and the coast-watcher would be captured and killed as a spy. After the 1941 capture, torture and murder of Percy Good, an elderly copra planter on Buka Island, off Bougainville, all civilians were enlisted into the RAN in the belief that their combatant status would protect them if they were captured by the enemy.

There was a bounty on the Coast-Watchers heads just like a PT-Skipper, but the japs would usually just kill the native and not pay off. This tactic just turned the rest of the native population against the japs, so their barbarism played in our favor, but we did lose some fine men because of it.

One big problem we had continually during the war was communicating with the bigger boys of our own Navy when we were out on patrol, they thought they were the rulers of the sea, and if they did not know you, then you must be the "enemy." They liked to shoot first and ask questions after the attack was over.

Mike was on patrol one night with another boat, and his buddy decided to go to the right around an island and Mike was going to stay to the left, but his lookout spotted two bow waves coming at him. He knew that his other boat would take about thirty minutes to come around the island, so it was either a couple of japs or it was his own Navy on patrol.

Our boats used a different radio frequency to be able to hear each other and stay out of the way of the bigger ships but tonight looked like trouble brewing. The two destroyers increased speed and headed right for Mike's boat.

He used the Morse lamp to try to alert them that he was one of the good guys, but to no avail, he even brought up the radio frequency for them, and he heard them chatting back and forth saying "it must be a jap patrol craft, we don't have anything that small out here".

After he heard that exchange, he came up on the radio and declared to them that he was a peter-tare (PT boat) from Tulagi and after the one skipper said "bullshit, let's go get him" Mike told them in plain English that "if you want your balls blown back to Dodger stadium, go for it!" Both ships slowed and changed course, nothing more came out of it.

The next morning at the briefing the Commander brought up the fact that some destroyer skippers were complaining of unprofessional use on the radio net, but nothing else was ever said about it.

The japs wanted Guadalcanal back, and they were sending ships down nightly to drop off soldiers and even naval-marines to help to take it back from what they originally were told was around 1000 soldiers. In fact, it was closer to 10,000 Marines of the First Marine Division, and they were there to stay.

In late December after my class graduated from Melville, I got promoted from Ensign to Lieutenant Junior Grade. Normal peacetime promotions would take years to come through but because of the war need they were bumping everyone up quicker.

7 Photo by US Navy- Provided by Wikipedia

For the first few weeks, while operating around the Eastern Solomon's, Mike never had a chance to fire a torpedo at a jap ship. He was shot at and bombed by our own Army Air Corps a few times. They would bomb and strafe without warning because they always thought it was a jap submarine on the surface, recharging their batteries, and if they took the time to do a fly-by to get a positive I.D., the "sub" would dive, and they would lose their "kill"

They would not even say they were sorry when he would bring it up at the Base Ops. There were plenty of fist fights when the PT-skipper would find the offending pilot the next day in the shower tent or mess tent. But the Army pilots would always declare that they had bombed a jap ship, or a jap sub the night before in their de-brief, they would never admit that they fired on a U.S. PT boat.

We actually lost some boats to "friendly" fire like that. I do not know how you could call that "friendly fire." If our boats fired on the offending plane, they would take that as confirmation that the boat was "the enemy" why else would they return fire.

At first, the japs were brazening in their dropping off men and supplies, and they would pull in to the beach and run the front of the freighters and troop ships aground and off-load the soldiers and their ammo supplies since we did not have any Navy to speak about. After the ship was empty, it would be lighter weight, and they would just back it into the current and sail away.

It took us a while to get the upper hand on the japs. They were really good in using their Long Lance Torpedoes, even at night. The japs had practiced night fighting tactics, and our Navy could not spare the money for anything other than a practice torpedo, and if you lost it during a practice shot, there was hell to pay.

The Long Lance was a big torpedo for its time, some two feet in diameter, almost thirty feet long and weighing almost three tons. It was armed with a 1,080-pound warhead that was fifty percent larger than most other torpedo warheads. Most important was the Long Lance's propulsion system. Most other nations had torpedoes propelled by steam, diesel or electric propulsion. But the Japanese opted for a pure oxygen-based system (inspired by an earlier British design) that could send the Long Lance out to twelve miles at a speed of forty-eight knots, or an incredible twenty-four miles—about the same range as a battleship's gun — at a speed of thirty-six knots. The Long Lance also didn't leave telltale bubbles on the surface to warn enemy ships a torpedo was approaching.

That is one reason we were losing so many navy ships at night during an at-sea battle with the enemy. They would fire their torpedo and stay on their course, and our ships would not know that enemy torpedoes were on the way, and they would run right into them. The jap navy relied on using human eye sight at the beginning of the war, they made their sailors eat a lot of greens and carrots, and it worked a lot better than the beef and potatoes diets of our sailors.

We, in the meantime, were trying to perfect the use of radar and sonar to find the enemy. At first, we had sonar installed on the boats to help us find an enemy submarine, but the units were no good with the speed of the boat. We had to come to a stop to be able to get a reading on anything in the water, and that just set you up for an attack by the enemy you were looking for. So we did away with sonar.

Finally, after we finally started sinking some of their troop ships and freighters around Guadalcanal, they started using fast destroyers to drop off barrels loaded with supplies in the water and let the barrels float ashore instead of stopping the ships.

The jap navy would sneak down to Guadalcanal and make a drop of supplies in barrels that would float ashore and beat feet out of the area before our boats could get organized and set up a trap.

Our boats that came upon any floating enemy barrels would pick up whatever they wanted to save and could carry and sink the rest. These added supplies only helped our guys. The rice and sake (rice wine) and dried fruits and veggies were the favorites, but there was only so much you could do with dried fish, so they usually went back into the water with holes in them to sink them.

Every so often they would find a dead sailor that had either fallen overboard or had gotten blown overboard, and they still had the kapok life preserver on them, if it was an enemy sailor, they would pull them close and cut off the preserver and let the ocean claim the body.

They were told that if it was a US service member, to save the dog-tags to turn in because the PT boats had no way to keep the body on-board for a proper burial. A few times they did bring them back to "Graves Registration" if they were on their way back to base to give them a proper burial.

Mike used to go out every night and try to find any destroyers that were running men and materials to the islands in his area. Usually, they struck out. They would go out for two to three weeks and never see any enemy ships at all, but then there would be six nights in a row that the japs would try to get men into Guadalcanal.

On the night of December14, at 02:00, Mike got a scramble notice to get underway immediately, this was supposed to be his first night off in almost a month, he went out after an intense night bombing of Henderson Field and was cruising between Tulagi and Guadalcanal when he was spotted by a Jap light cruiser north of him with a bone in its teeth. He turned in to set up a firing solution for a torpedo attack and got tunnel vision. After he fired his full load of fish, Mike never saw the destroyer that was coming from the south to re-join with his cruiser, two of his fish missed but two others made a good hit amidships on the light cruiser. It took three hours for his cruiser to sink, but he never saw the fish hit its mark because the destroyer coming at him cut his boat in half.

The explosion was seen for ten miles, and nobody survived either the blast or the ramming by the ship. Other boats made a sweep of the area and reported some small pieces of burnt wood but no bodies. I was finishing my training at Melville, R.I. waiting for my turn to go to the Pacific when I got a message that Mike was killed on December 14, 1942.

We had made a lot of plans together, for during the war and after it was over, but they would never get to see the light of day. I would miss my brother deeply, but I would make those jap bastards pay for what they had done.

My Squadron #5 (twelve boats) were sent to Panama to get ready for our boat trip to the South Pacific, but the Commander of the Panama Sea Frontier said that he thought that squadron-2 should be sent ahead and keep the new squadron-5 at Panama for extra training. I guess that we did not meet his expectations for being "ready" for war.

They split up our squadron like they did to Mike, six of our boats-PT's 109 to 114 were sent on with the original boats from Squadron-2 to Tulagi and arrived at the end of January 1943. I got to stay in Panama for now.

Now I buckled down and drove my crew like a man with a mission, we needed to become the best we could be so we could get released to go to war. I had my torpedo men work on our torpedoes after everyone else had gone back to the barracks and stopped for the night.

Our Gunners-mates had to tear down every gun and re-oil them at the end of the day. I reminded them that to much oil was as much a bad thing as to little oil. I had the Boatswain-mates paint another coat on the boat so it would stay looking good and the Electrician-mate double-checked all the electric circuits to look for any shorts that could cause a problem later.

I put a lock on the fuel filling port after a few boats reported finding wax in their fuel tanks from sabotage and I told the crew that if any vandalism was done on their watch to my boat, I would personally man the firing squad.

They got on their toes after that threat, and they knew that I meant it. They even doubled the manpower on duty to make sure nothing happened to our boat. We were ready for action, and everyone knew it.

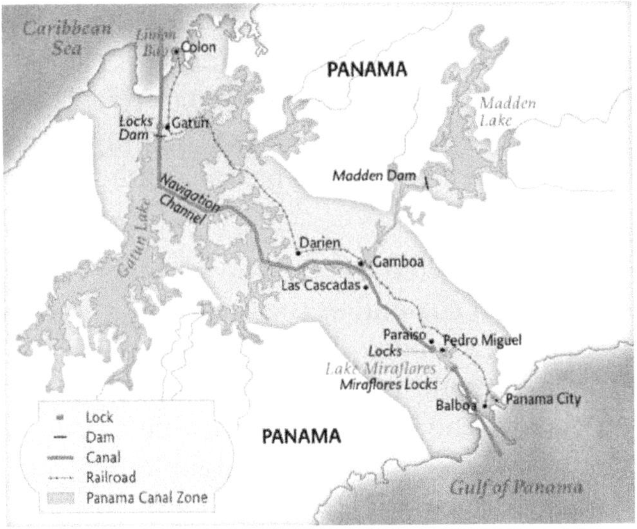

#8 Map provided by Wikipedia

We spent every waking minute running around the canal zone, from the Atlantic Ocean thru the freshwater lake (Gatun Lake) all the way to the Pacific Ocean. We escorted fuel tankers and troop transports and even new Destroyers through on their way to the war.

All our large major combat ships were built so that they would fit through the Panama Canal Locks, Battleships and Carriers, all had to fit, nothing could be wider than 108 feet at the widest part nor longer than 1000 feet in length.

It was sobering to realize that a lot of the men that were waving to us from the troop transports would not be coming home again, they would die and be buried on some forgotten island, thousands of miles from their loved ones.

We spent many a day making practice torpedo runs on all the ships that came through the canal. We went all the way out to the Galapagos in the Pacific and practiced our star shooting for navigation after sunset and then returned to our base until sunrise and did it all over again the next day, and the next day, there was no weekends off anymore.

There were a few times that we would pull out of the way of the shipping and beach the boat when we were in the freshwater lake (Gatun Lake) in the middle of the canal and actually take a bath in the fresh water and wash out some uniforms and lay them out on the deck to dry out. We were far enough away from the ships that they could not see what we were doing.

It was relaxing to take a couple of hours to rest and wash our uniforms out, they were working us so much that nobody had the extra time to do their laundry, if anyone at the headquarters asked why it took us so long to get back, I just told them I went further out with our ships to make sure there were no jap subs stalking them. It would never go any further than that.

After a few hours rest we would get back to the war routine and line up with another group to escort from the Atlantic Ocean to the Pacific, it would take us a full day to move one group of ships at a time.

We would pick up a couple of ships on the Atlantic side and ride along with them through the different locks, they had to be pulled thru by these mini-trains that ran on rails beside the locks and were connected by cables to the ships. This kept the ship from running into the gates at the end of the locks. The largest ships even had to use fleet tugs to maneuver through the Gatun Lake area since sometimes you would come upon opposing traffic.

While in the locks it was one-way traffic only on each side, so you did not have to worry about running into any other ship, but in the freshwater lake the smaller ships could start their engines and propel themselves.

Every day was the same thing, it never stopped. The ship traffic ran every day and every night, rain or shine just like the mailman back home, but we did not have snow or sleet to contend with like they did. We only had to watch out for enemy attacks.

After we left the Canal-Zone, we were given a certificate that we had gone through it.

#8A- Photo by author

Chapter 3 - Polly-Wogs in the Pacific

We got lucky when Squadron-7 came down to Panama, they looked worse than we did when we got there so, they were notified that we would be replacing them on the trip to the South Pacific and they would take over the security of the Canal Zone. They would train like we did until someone else happens to come down to the canal that looks worse than they did.

The base commander notified us to be ready to move out on Friday, they were building special shipping cradles to hold our boats on top of three different freighters. We got loaded on Thursday and got to sea, on Friday afternoon around 16:00, we passed the Pacific Perimeter and waved good-bye to our PT boat escorts.

We had been to sea for a day when the ship's Captain came on the one MC announcing system and told us that on Sunday morning, we would be crossing the Equator and that we would be participating in the time-honored Naval Tradition of "Crossing the Line" into "King Neptune's Domain."

The new sailors that had never crossed the line were called "Polly-Wogs," and the men that had already "crossed the line" on a previous trip were called "Shellbacks," and we were told that everything that we went through was done in fun and that "Rank did not have any privileges."

At reveille at 06:00 on Sunday morning we had to wear our clothes inside out and crawl on our hands and knees while we were being butt-whipped by men dressed up as pirates and wielding three-foot sections of firehose that were made into whips. The shellbacks were having a lot of fun at our expense. We even had to visit the "Royal Barber" for a hair-cut, I am glad that my hair grows fast!

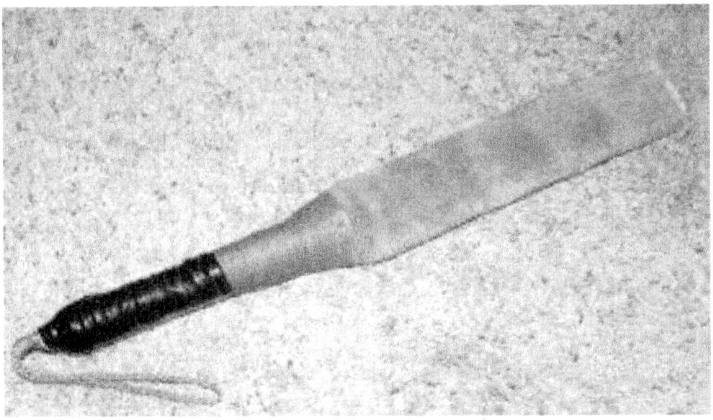

#9 Photo by Author

#9A Photo courtesy of Author

You were told not to look up at a shellback because you had not earned it yet, you were smacked on your butt at every turn of the journey. For breakfast, we had to eat green spaghetti and hot sauced scrambled eggs, burnt toast, and black grits off our trays that were put on the deck. You had to eat without knives or forks because again, we had not earned the use of utensils yet, so you slurped it up.

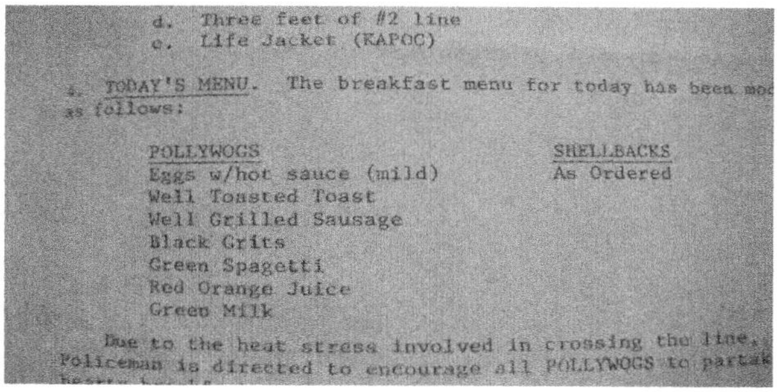

d. Three feet of #2 line
e. Life Jacket (KAPOC)

TODAY'S MENU. The breakfast menu for today has been mod as follows:

POLLYWOGS	SHELLBACKS
Eggs w/hot sauce (mild)	As Ordered
Well Toasted Toast	
Well Grilled Sausage	
Black Grits	
Green Spagetti	
Red Orange Juice	
Green Milk	

Due to the heat stress involved in crossing the line, Policeman is directed to encourage all POLLYWOGS to partak

Photo #10 by author

They spread sand on the deck, and we had to "sweep" the dirt up with our butts into piles. Then they would spread it back out for the next sailor. The "shellbacks" would laugh and taunt us at every step, you had to laugh at what we all were going through in order to make it through the day.

This was a long day, but it was all worth it in the end, it made me want to go through it from a shellback position some day in the near future. I would remember this day for the rest of my life that was for sure.

We had to go before "The Royal Court" and beg for forgiveness for being a "Polly-Wog."

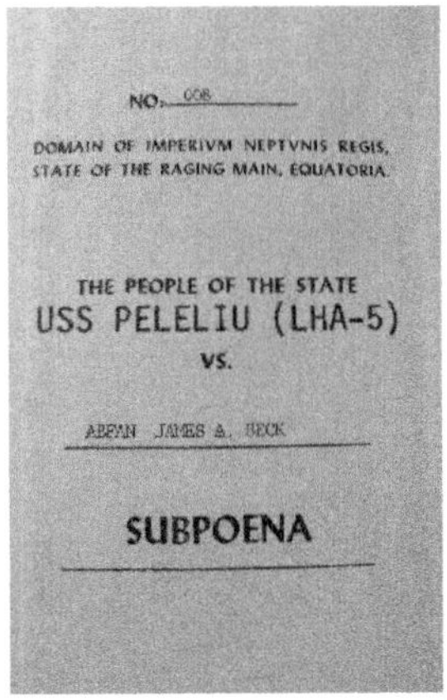
NO. 008

DOMAIN OF IMPERIVM NEPTVNIS REGIS,
STATE OF THE RAGING MAIN, EQUATORIA.

THE PEOPLE OF THE STATE
USS PELELIU (LHA-5)
VS.

ABFAN JAMES A. BECK

SUBPOENA

Photo #10A By Author

My crimes against "King Neptune" were listed as:

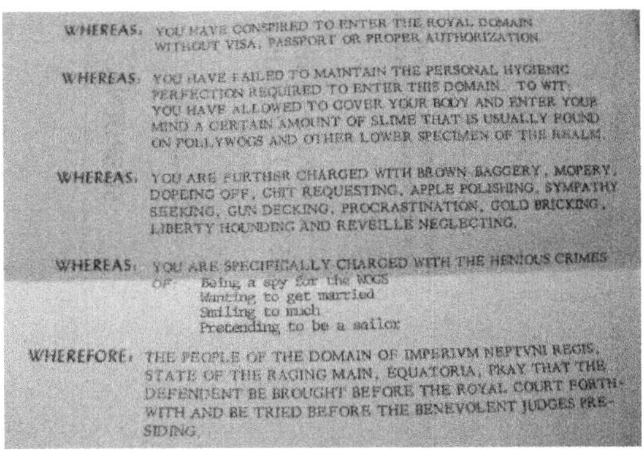
WHEREAS: YOU HAVE CONSPIRED TO ENTER THE ROYAL DOMAIN WITHOUT VISA, PASSPORT OR PROPER AUTHORIZATION.

WHEREAS: YOU HAVE FAILED TO MAINTAIN THE PERSONAL HYGIENIC PERFECTION REQUIRED TO ENTER THIS DOMAIN. TO WIT: YOU HAVE ALLOWED TO COVER YOUR BODY AND ENTER YOUR MIND A CERTAIN AMOUNT OF SLIME THAT IS USUALLY FOUND ON POLLYWOGS AND OTHER LOWER SPECIMEN OF THE REALM.

WHEREAS: YOU ARE FURTHER CHARGED WITH BROWN BAGGERY, MOPERY, DOPEING OFF, CHIT REQUESTING, APPLE POLISHING, SYMPATHY SEEKING, GUN DECKING, PROCRASTINATION, GOLD BRICKING, LIBERTY HOUNDING AND REVEILLE NEGLECTING.

WHEREAS: YOU ARE SPECIFICALLY CHARGED WITH THE HENIOUS CRIMES OF: Being a spy for the WOGS
Wanting to get married
Smiling to much
Pretending to be a sailor

WHEREFORE: THE PEOPLE OF THE DOMAIN OF IMPERIVM NEPTVNI REGIS, STATE OF THE RAGING MAIN, EQUATORIA, PRAY THAT THE DEFENDENT BE BROUGHT BEFORE THE ROYAL COURT FORTHWITH AND BE TRIED BEFORE THE BENEVOLENT JUDGES PRESIDING.

Photo #10B By Author

I was convicted as charged and sentenced to five minutes in the stockade. We all got "shots" in the butt from the "Royal Doctor" and boy did they sting, You had to crawl in front of the fattest "Chief" that was dressed up as a "Royal Baby" wearing an over-sized diaper, they had smeared this oily, greasy, concoction that had hot sauce in it on his belly and you had to kiss it. You would try to get away with a little "peck," but he was ready for you.

Photo #11 of the author with the Royal Baby

The "Royal Baby" would grab your head and rub your face all over his belly. Then you were taken to a tube that was filled with old garbage and stunk to "High Heaven," and you had to crawl through it, the whole time you were getting beat by the paddles.

Photo #12 by the author

After the "shit-tube" you were taken to a tub and baptized into "The realm of King Neptune." I was officially a Shell-back, and an entry would be entered into my naval service record showing the date and time and the actual coordinates of the crossing. From now on I would be the beater and not the beaten.

Photo #13 by the author

We had to strip down on the fantail and throw our soiled clothes away, they had set up a couple of firehoses so that we could take a saltwater shower and try to get clean. After our showers, we got to put on our regular uniforms, and they did a special supper for the officers in the wardroom. We were learning what the term "ship-mate" really meant. The crew got to eat steak and lobster that night to celebrate the crossing.

Our three freighters were part of a group of fourteen ships that had left the Canal together, there were freighters and tankers and a couple of troop ships that were in route to the South West Pacific. We had six destroyers to babysit us during the trip. We had different alerts every day, most of them turned out to be a whale, or a log that was seen by an inexperienced ship lookout and the destroyers would give chase until they could confirm it was not a submarine or a periscope.

We went to General Quarters every morning at 05:00 and every afternoon at 18:00 because we had been told that the japs liked to attack in the glare of the sun so you could not see them coming.

We were about three days out of New Caledonia, and the sun was just coming up, we were at G.Q. just like normal, we never saw the torpedoes coming, they hit the freighter on our port side and a fuel tanker loaded with aviation gasoline ahead of him. The tanker blew up in one single boom and disintegrated into pieces that fell back on fire, burning on the water, the jap was hidden in the glare of the sun-rise, and we could not see him.

He was on the east side of the group, we had a jap submarine this time, not a whale that was running with us and he was trying to pick us off. The destroyers went into action, and two of them ran down what they thought was the suspected torpedo track, and they started dropping "depth-charges."

A depth-charge was like a big metal trash can that was packed with around 250 pounds of TNT and a small charge that went off at a pre-set depth that would then blow up the can. The hope was that it would go off just under the offending enemy sub and the force of the explosion would break the sub and either force them to the surface or sink them.

The freighter started sinking from the stern, and the skipper called out to "Abandon Ship" so the crew was busy getting the lifeboats lowered into the water. Our PT-crews did not want to lose their boats so disobeying orders they manned the boats and cut away the straps holding the boats into the shipping cradles.

As the ship was going down, the rising water allowed the four PT boats to float clear of the freighter. They were able to start the engines and back away from the sinking ship so as not to get caught in the vortex caused when the ship went down. All the PT boats assisted in rescuing any Merchant Marine sailors in the water and took them over to another freighter that took them on-board.

The PT boats would have to either be towed or make their own way to port over the next three days. The waves got so high at one time that you would see the PT boat when he was on the crest, but he would all but disappear when he went down into the trough of the wave.

The destroyers thought they had sunk the sub, but we all believed they only scared him deep since we never saw any evidence of sinking. He might come back, so everyone was on high alert for the rest of the trip.

We made it to New Caledonia and off-loaded the rest of the boat's pier-side. We were then pulled by a couple of oilers for the next part of our trip, we left the next day and got to within 300 miles of the Guadalcanal area and then were told to go the rest of the way under our own power, they made sure our tanks were topped off before we pulled away.

This area was already known as "Torpedo Alley" and for a good cause, because many allied ships had been sunk by jap subs in this part of the war zone. The ships wanted to be able to move independently if any enemy subs or ships or planes appeared. They did not want to be tied down with a cable to six PT boats. They needed to be able to zig-zag and turn quickly if they came under attack and being tied to six PT boats did not give them time to react and disconnect the towing cables before the bombs would fall around them.

The skipper would see the bombers coming in, and when the bombs would be released he would have maybe sixty seconds to react and turn the ship to try to make the bomb miss from a direct hit, even a close-aboard miss could do a lot of damage to a ship, it could rupture the hull and cause flooding under the water-line and that could sink your ship if your damage control was not up to snuff. And when you were working with Merchant Seamen who never trained instead of regular Navy Sailors that trained every day for things like this. This war was starting to get real to all of us now.

Chapter 4 - Stopping at Tulagi

We got to Tulagi around the end of March 1943 and was told that we would be heading north very shortly so to not bother getting settled in.

In reality, it took us about six months and a few different island stop-overs to make it to the Russel Islands on our way to Rendova Harbor. They sent us out on daily excursions to hunt for any jap ships that were trying to come down the slot. Most days we never found anything while we were out running around.

We would always get the boats underway whenever an air-raid sounded so that we would not get caught tied up to the pier and be a sitting duck. I saw the remains of a few boats that ended up getting bombed at the pier. The sailors tried to shoot at the attacking planes but one of our biggest advantages of being a small, fast boat was being able to change directions quicker than the plane that was attacking us could, and our machine guns could follow him where ever he went in the sky around us. If the boat was pier-side, then he was a motionless target just waiting to get tagged by a jap plane.

My next promotion made it to our next base before I did, so now I was a full Lieutenant, maybe these faster promotions were a sign of what was to come, or they might be a sign that the other officers were getting killed by the enemy, instead of me being "better" than all the others, as I thought.

#14 Map provided by Wikipedia

The “Tokyo Express” as we had learned to call them, would at first bring troop transports loaded with soldiers and they would always bring a few heavy cruisers and destroyers to shell the Marines at Henderson field on “Cactus” so that the “Cactus-Air Force” could not come up against them. That was the code-name (Cactus) given by the brass for Guadalcanal.

At first there were fifty fighters and twenty-five bombers assigned to “Cactus”, Admiral King in Washington, D.C. had allocated those planes to be dropped off by the Navy so, Admiral Nimitz in Hawaii sent the Aircraft Carrier-Hornet to drop the aircraft at Guadalcanal and then they went back to Hawaii to get a new squadron assigned to the ship. Most of those planes dropped off had been destroyed in the first two weeks after they were flown in.

Our military air command in the Guadalcanal area was a hodge-podge accumulation of equipment. We had a few different types of planes (fighters, bombers, scouts) from different ships and even different countries, if their ships were either sunk or damaged by the japs and had to leave the area for repairs, they would off-load any aircraft they had before they left the area and they would be assigned to provide air security for "Cactus".

The japs always tried to hit our bases at night with their heavy cruisers and battleships, one reason why the jap ships liked to hit our bases after dark was that they knew that our planes were daytime fighters for the most part.

We could launch our fighters before dark, but they would not be able to land after dark, or they would crash and burn during the landing attempt so the japs would come in after dark every few nights and shell the crap out of Henderson field and any aircraft they could hit.

It seemed that the japs were getting pretty good at destroying our aircraft on the ground, there were a few times that fifteen out of the twenty available planes would get hit by these sixteen-inch shells from the jap battleships and blow them to pieces, these big shells were the size of a small sedan and weighed over 2000 pounds each.

So, we had the Seabees, a group of professional construction men from all the different trades, there were pipe-fitters, equipment operators, mechanics, contractors, etc. that was just formed by the US Navy. This Construction Battalion started building revetments to protect the aircraft when they were parked. With a plane in the revetments, if one was damaged by a bomb blast, the one next to it would be protected from the shrapnel that went flying through the air. They also used the bulldozers to make roads wide enough that the planes could hide further back in the jungle so that they all would not get damaged during an air-raid or a shelling from the jap ships

Sometimes our mechanics could save different parts from the wrecked planes and cannibalize the parts they could save to patch up another plane that needed those parts. The base commander was always sending a message to SWPAC-Command that the available aircraft or fuel was destroyed in the latest enemy raid and they needed more delivered right away.

They would try to send a freighter pulling a fuel barge with a destroyer escort but somedays they would have to fight their way close enough to the island where any available aircraft could fly out to protect them if possible. At this time, we did not have air superiority, the japs would fly planes down at any time to see if they could bomb or strafe anything in the area.

The japs would send out aircraft to look for any fuel barges or freighters trying to make it to the island to unload the supplies and fuel they were carrying, and they would bomb the ships and strafe any survivors they found in lifeboats. It could take an oiler three to four days to make the trip, and if the enemy saw them, they would radio in the last position and what time they were last spotted and then any jap bomber around would know where they were and where they were going.

We even sent subs to the island with fifty-five-gallon barrels lashed to the topsides, and they would only go to forty feet deep to try to sneak in and off-load the fuel.

It was rare that our fleet would try to fight back at the beginning of the war. The few times that our destroyers tried to come out and fight, they usually got beat up pretty bad. We lost quite a few ships and hundreds of sailors in the first few battles around Savo Island.

It got so bad that the Navy started calling the bay around Guadalcanal and Tulagi Island the "The Iron Bottom Bay." The Marines on the islands would set on the beach at night watching the sea-battles and hope that the U.S. was winning this time, but they knew the truth when come sunrise, there were U.S. Navy sailors and not japs floating dead in the waters surrounding the island.

We learned early on to always go out in pairs, so when we went out on nightly patrols looking for enemy ships, we usually just got chased by our own ships, someone always forgot to let the big boys know that they had some smaller cousins in the area also.

One night we were told that some destroyers were coming down "The Slot" so we got under-way about 21:00 and hid in the shadows on the south-east side of Kolombangara Island until they pulled up.

There were two of us waiting to spring the "ambush" on the japs, but at the same time as we saw their bow waves cutting through the water, we came under fire from two fast destroyers that had snuck in around the north side of the island! It looks like the japs had their own ambush set up for us this time.

We had to go to full speed ahead and start some fancy maneuvers to be able to get out of this one without getting hit by any of the three-inch cannon fire that was being thrown at us.

I really thought our numbers were up that night, but we came out of it without even a splinter, we did not get to fire any torpedoes that night, and there were going to be many more nights like this one.

One night we were out on a patrol when the clouds just opened up on us, it was refreshing, but it was one of those, you could not see your hands in front of your face type of rain. It lasted about fifteen minutes, and when we came out of it, we saw another PT boat come running around the northern end of this island we were sitting near. I had pulled into a little cove to wait out the downpour. We could hear this guy's engines going full out, and sure enough, he was being chased by a jap fast-attack destroyer. Those things could do thirty knots easily, and this poor guy was losing the race.

I told everyone to man their battle-stations, and for the engine-room to give me full speed ahead, we had to help this guy out. We pulled out after them and started gaining on the destroyer. They were running full out and zig-zagging to throw off the shell fire from the three-inch guns so we could not get set up for a torpedo shot. I decided to pull up as close as we could and let him have some of our .50 cal., and even some of the anti-aircraft shots. I told the crew to aim for the bridge area and to hit any guns they saw.

The chase ran for another ten minutes and then we had our chance to hit him with all the machine guns. He made a quick turn to the left and decided that he did not like the odds anymore, he did not know if we were leading him into a trap or not.

The other Peter-tare came back alongside us, and we chatted for a few minutes, he had been on patrol for the last seven hours and was thinking of going for home when the destroyer came around the southern edge of the island and started to chase him. It was all he could do to keep out of the range-finders and not become kindling wood.

I told him that we had just happened to pull in and come to a stop because of that downpour or we would have missed them completely. The skipper said that the drinks were on him tonight when we got back to the PT-Base, and to look him up, his name was Kennedy, and his boat was the 109.

We had stopped the transports from coming to "The Canal" now, by sinking a few around the island. So they started using fast destroyers to try to take their men off the island. They would send a few ships to keep us busy, while a few extra destroyers would slip into the beach area and take off a few hundred soldiers. By February 1, 1943, the exodus was over.

After the japs pulled their people off of Guadalcanal and gave ownership over to the United States Marines, we did not have any more ships running all the way to the end of "the slot," they started using barges instead of destroyers to try to out-smart us and hide from us.

One night we were cruising around some islands on one engine with the mufflers on so we could hear anything around us. My Quartermaster 1st.class Bill Adams from California was steering the boat when he said, "All stop!"

I asked him what he saw. He said there looks to be a sub sitting in the channel ahead of us. He had a really good night vision, so I took his word at it.

I used the binoculars, and I could just barely make out an outline about 1500 yards ahead of us, there was an island behind us that would keep us in the shadows of the mountain from the jap viewpoint. We could hear them using a hammer and see a welder's torch once in a while. I bet they had damaged a forward plane that was used to dive the sub like water wings.

I told Adams I wish I had eaten more carrots when I was younger! We set up the torpedo with a six-foot depth, and we fired one from a dead stop. It ran hot and true for about forty-five seconds and hit him square amidships right at the conning tower. He blew up in the middle, and both ends went up at a forty-five-degree angle and slid under the waves. I had a camera with me, so I took a few pictures as proof of the sinking, we rode over to see if there were any survivors, there was none. We did scoop up a few floating items to help us identify the number of the sub we had just killed.

It was deep in the channel, so the wreckage was already down far enough; it would not be a navigation hazard. Then Adams asked me if the sub was disabled, did I think that another sub might come this way to help him?

I told him it would be worth the wait to see since we were striking out just cruising around, so we pulled back closer to the island behind us and put out a sea-anchor to keep us from floating ashore.

We only had to wait about three hours, and sure enough, a larger "mother" sub came floating along at a nice slow pace looking for his wounded chick. I bet this was one of those "cows" that we had heard about, they were like a small combination of a fuel tanker and sub tender. They carried mechanics and spare parts and thousands of gallons of extra fuel to be able to refuel a submarine while it was out on patrol or fix an engine casualty if they had one.

The only thing they did not carry was torpedoes, the extra room was converted from a torpedo room to big fuel tanks. She came to a stop in about the same position as the first sub had been before we hit her. We pulled in our sea-anchor and started toward her on one muffled engine, this time I fired two torpedoes at her, one to the conning tower and one in front of her just-in-case she got underway.

Sure enough, the lookouts were alert and saw the first torpedo heading their way, so they got under-way trying to make the fish miss them aft. This put them right in the path of the second torpedo, it hit in the front of the sub, it must have hit their extra fuel storage because the resulting explosion blew the sub to pieces. I almost did not have time to bring up the camera for a quick picture.

Because of the extra fuel onboard, there was a big fireball and lots of burning fuel on the surface of the water. If there had been any survivors, they would have been burned alive trying to swim away from the sinking sub.

It was rare to find a submarine on the surface, but tonight we had found and killed two subs in the same area. It was time to skedaddle and clear the area because the fires would keep any other enemy ships or subs from coming into this channel for some time to come.

We started meeting more barges at night than destroyers or troop transports after a while. I would line up for a perfect torpedo shot and fire it, and nothing would happen at the appointed time, one of our main problems with barge hunting was that our torpedoes went right under the barge due to the shallow draft of the barge and exploded on the beach past them.

We had to start using guns to go after the barges, this tactic worked for a while but once they started using armor on the barge sides even the .50 cal. machine guns just bounced off the sides.

The japs started loading the barges with all kind of weapons and with the 100 enemy soldiers they could carry that just added to their amount of fire-power they could throw our way. One night we were out during a rainstorm and visibility was like only one boat-length, so we were moving really slow trying to find the enemy.

All of a sudden, we found ourselves in the middle of a group of barges slogging away in the rain. We opened fire with every gun we had, and the barges fired back with everything they had. It would have been easier if we could have just ducked and let them shoot each other. Our .50 cal. bullets just bounced off the armor sides of the barges, we needed a different plan. So, this is one time we tucked our tails and ran for our lives, to be able to fight another day.

We ended up putting an Army 37 mm. Anti-Tank gun attached to two by six wood boards on the bow of the boat to keep it from flying off whenever we fired it, we moved the bow .50 cal. back toward the rear of the radio mast.

We went to Woodlark Island for some time and operated out of a hidden cove, and we intercepted a large number of armored barges moving between the islands. The japs found that they could sneak around the islands during the night and it was harder to find them in the shallows, if they saw us, they would beach the barge and run into the jungle until we were gone, then they would re-load the troops and start out again.

We would use the Anti-Tank gun and just blow the barge out of the water, or we could call in air support, if they were available, they could drop a couple of 250 pounders on the barge. Some of the barges were loaded to the gills with ammo, and the fireworks shows we saw were better than anything we ever saw back home for the 4th of July.

Then we could mark the island for bombing and shelling from our "Big Ships" or the Army bombers to get the soldiers that ran into the jungle.

They kept sending us out at night to look for jap ships that might be trying to run troops down to the islands at night, we were supposed to be working one night on, and one night off, but you know how that goes. We had a tough night and were looking forward to a night off when they let us know we were needed to fill in for another PT boat that had an engine casualty. Two boats were going out, but we would separate and go two different directions.

We went out in his place, we had been out about four hours just cruising between the different islands when everything quit, the engines just shut down, I mean cold. The motor-macs said they checked everything, and nothing was out of place. The electrician checked all the wiring and said there was just no juice flowing.

We had to fire up the emergency generator to get enough power to radio our base that we were broke down and needed a tow, we gave them our map coordinates, and they said to wait for a reply. They got back to us in a few minutes and said that another PT would be diverted and come our way. The radio operator then said not to go anywhere!

Such a joker, he could do stand-up comedy at the local Holiday Inn on Friday nights. We told him we would be here unless a taxi happened by. We had floated over to an island and put out our sea-anchor, it was almost an hour before the tow got to us, by then we were more than ready to go home. They pulled up to us and threw us a line that we made fast on the bow cleat, and we took the next five hours to get pulled home.

The Enginemen still had no idea by the time we got home to base, so the PT-Tender sent a couple of guys over to help. It took them about another four hours to troubleshoot and when they pushed the starter button it turned over as if there was no problem. You know how every navy ship takes on a persona of its own? Well, I guess that she was just telling us that she was tired and needed a break. The next morning, we found out that while our boat was out of action the night before, that over 1000 enemy troops were off-loaded on an island we were intending on invading, now it would be a little tougher when we did go in.

Usually, if we did not make it back to our base before daylight, we would stop in a cove and pull in under some hanging trees. We would stretch out a camouflage net and take a siesta during the day when we were most vulnerable to air attack by jap snoopers.

The cook would fish off the stern sometimes so we could have some fried fish for dinner if we wanted to.

It was important for good crew morale to have a cook that actually knew how to cook for us. The Navy would not assign an actual cook to a PT boat because they were in such high demand throughout the Navy. Would you rather make 500 guys happy on a big ship or just fourteen guys on a PT Boat?

Sometimes the guys would take turns cooking to rotate the chore. I had a guy one time that the only thing he knew how to make was either Peanut Butter and Jelly sandwiches or Pancakes.

Photo #15 US Navy PT Museum – Provided by Wikipedia

I once had a real cook that had been cooking at a fancy San Diego restaurant for three years after he went to chef's school and when the war started, he joined the Navy. He never told them he was a cook when he came in, so they made him a Boatswain Mate, so he chipped paint and repainted whatever he had just chipped, this is called "corrosion control" in the US Navy. In the real world, it is just called "busy work."

He could cook anything the crew could think of. One time I had to tell him to stop using grenades to fish since the sound could give us away if there were any enemy soldiers on the island.

He asked me if there was any way that we could get an oven made for him to be able to bake bread and dinner rolls? I asked him if pizza was included in that, and he said yes sir if you can get me the ingredients, I can make it for you. I told him I might just be able to do that. I was thinking of asking the local Sea-Bee commander, but I had to be careful that our secret did not get out to the wrong hands.

First, I would have to arrange for a couple of boxes of chocolate bars. I knew some Marines that had some jap souvenirs they had come upon after the japs vacated the island ahead of the invasion. If I could get the Seabees to let loose another ice machine I could trade that for the souvenirs, then I could get the chocolate bars for the guys to make me the oven and we could have a pizza night minus the movie.

This cook was great, we would have baked ham and sweet potatoes one day, and then ham sandwiches for the next day. He did roast beef and baked potatoes with handmade rolls. He even surprised me with a birthday cake for my birthday!

He was with us for about six months until one of the crew happened to mention to a friend on shore that our cook could make "Baked Alaskan." That was all it took, and he was transferred to the base and made to cook for the Base Commander, we went back to PB & J and pancakes again.

The Gunners Mates in charge of the guns would use this downtime to clean and oil the guns, and both Enginemen would use this time to tune up the engines so we could get another five knots out of her if needed.

These boats would not shift by themselves like a civilian motorboat from forward to reverse, so there had to be an Engineman on duty at all times in the engine room to physically shift to forward or reverse or to put all three engines on line for all ahead full or even all stop. We would call down a voice-tube to tell him what we wanted to do. If you pushed the throttles full ahead from slow cruising speed, you would usually flood the engines out, and you had to wait for the Engineman to re-start all the engines. This could be a big problem if an enemy ship was coming out of a rain-squall and you just saw him.

There was NO air conditioning in the engine room so sometimes the temps would get up over 120-130 degrees so the two enginemen would swap out after an hour working the engines. If we were moving, they were able to get some ventilation from these small vents mounted on the hull, and there was a big vent opening at the rear that had a ladder in it, and it was opened to the rear to allow heat to escape from the below deck engine area. That is also how they climbed in and out of the engine-room.

If you were off watch, I tried to encourage the men to go below to the bunk room and try to get some sleep, but it was warm all the time, and the riding of the waves did not help any.

One night when we were on a normal patrol, we got a coded message, my radioman decoded it, and we found out that two enemy cruisers and four jap destroyers were making a run on New Georgia tonight and we were to meet up with other boats for a coordinated attack. It was a good thing that we had refueled and had full tanks because we needed to run full out to make it to the meeting place in time. The boat was ready in all respects, the crew was ready and so was I.

I really wanted a jap destroyer silhouette painted on the cabin, it did not matter if it was the one that killed my brother Mike and his crew or not. As long as it was an enemy destroyer, I would be happy. There were four boats that were able to meet up just after dusk, so we planned to ride together up toward Johnston Point on the western tip of New Georgia.

At about 01:00, we saw flashes to the North-West of our location, so we headed that way loaded for bear.

It was pitch black this night, no moon, no stars but we knew where the island was, and the japs were throwing everything but the kitchen sink on their ships from the five-inch up to the ten-inch on the soldiers that occupied the Island of New Georgia.

We could see the white flashes from the smaller destroyers and the longer orange flashes from the eight and ten-inch salvos from the heavy cruisers, but there was so much smoke we could not see the ships until they fired their big guns. We needed to make a positive I.D. on the enemy ships since we were not sure if there were any friendlies in the area.

The smoke was so thick from the jap shelling and the big gunfire that we drove through the enemy formation and started receiving fire before we could even identify the ships. They were japs that we were sure of by now, there were two heavy-cruisers supported by four fast destroyers.

The destroyers started using their machine guns firing in all directions, and the Jap admiral on one of the Cruisers must have called them off because abruptly they stopped firing all around us. This gave us a break we needed to get closer to make sure our fish made good hits, we lined up at 500 yards to shoot in front of the lead cruiser and let two fish go, to impale themselves under the front stack and the rear of the ship.

My first torpedo must have hit the ship under the rack of depth-charges, because the resulting explosion blew the stern right off, all the way up to the rear stack. The fish that hit under the stack must have flooded the forward engine room because the ship lost all power and headway really quick. It was settling by the stern, and I could see sailors jumping into the water from every level.

I had lost the other jap ships during the encounter and out of the smoke came a destroyer that sliced the back 1/3rd of my boat off behind the radio mast, taking the engine room with them. The rest of us were tossed into the water that was covered with 100 octane fuel.

I do not think that the japs were aware that they had hit us during all the excitement. If the japs had known that they had hit us they could have fried us by firing a flare into the water, lucky for us that they kept on going, ten of us were picked up by another boat within thirty minutes.

We lost both Enginemen and both Torpedomen in the crash. We never found the Motor-Mac's bodies but the Torpedomen were thrown about fifty feet away from the rest of the boat that was still floating. We swam over and pulled them back to the bow. The rest of the boat stayed afloat because the crew had secured the water-tight doors when we got under-way.

One of the other boats came by and picked us up, and we went back to the base. I was going to have to write my first letters home to a crewman's family explaining how they died. It was not going to be easy.

We were taken to the base at New Georgia and turned over to the Corpsman and Doctors to provide first-aid. We arraigned for the burial of the two Torpedomen, and we had two guys that were in bad shape and were flown out to Australia to recuperate and then they would be flown back to the States. The rest of us only needed a little time off to recuperate from cuts and scrapes and dry out.

I went into the base operations shack the next morning asking how soon we could get assigned to another boat and the Commander said "Hell, my boy you just got fished out last night. Let's give it a couple of days and then come back to see me when you can walk straight".

I guess I was walking kind of sideways, even for a sailor. I had taken a wallop on the side of my head on the radio mast when I was thrown off the boat, and I figured a headache was the smallest of my worries.

The Dr. said I might have a slight concussion, and I needed to rest for a few days, My X.O. had a broken arm, so he was going to be beached for at least four to six weeks. Our S1c. Boatswain Mate got promoted to Chief and got orders to Melville, R.I. to train new personnel. The rest of the crew would wait for a new boat or be re-assigned and split-up among other boats.

I took three days off sunning myself during the day and running for a foxhole each night when the japs came a calling trying to shell the base. We had gotten smarter in the last two weeks and had moved all the vital support base personal about a mile inland, and basically, the base was an empty shell that got shelled for no reason by the japs.

Three days later the base operation officer saw me coming and said, "Hey, I got some good news for you. There is a boat at the island of Vella LaVella that needs a new skipper and a few new guys to help man it."

That meant that I would be taking over a boat that had just lost not only their skipper but three other men that they all had lived with and trained with for the last year. I said yes, we will take it.

We would be going in by submarine since this was not even a forward base yet, it was a secret stop off location that had been set up to help rescue downed airmen or coastwatchers that needed to be moved out if the japs were on their trail, supplies were airdropped or brought in at night by separate PT boats until we secured the other islands close by and wiped out those jap garrisons.

This also gave us a chance to hit any jap ships that might come down the slot at night, and we could slip in and pick off the last one in line before they knew what hit them. That plan worked more than once, the japs were slow to pick up on what we were doing to them.

Over a month's time, we sank five different transport ships loaded with "Sons of Nippon" that wanted to die for their "Emperor-Hirohito." It was nice to know that they would never be able to fire a shot at any of our Marines that were coming up the Solomon Ladder after them.

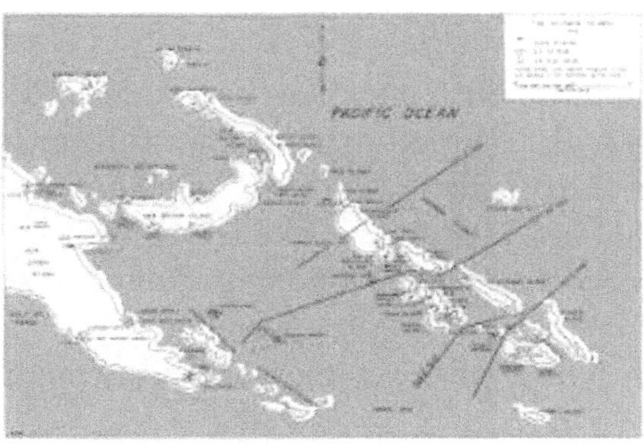

#16 map provided by Wikipedia

Chapter 5 - On to Vella-LaVella

We met up with the USS Seawitch in the channel between two islands south of us, one of the other boats in our squadron took us and bid farewell to us when they pulled up close aboard, we took a small boat over to the sub and waved good-bye to our friends.

The ride in the sub was kind of scary and interesting at the same time, we took the long road to get to Vella-LaVella so as to throw off any jap that might have seen us get on board the sub. There were no complaints from my crew when it came to the quality of food served to the submariners, they really did get the best food that went to the fleet. That night we had pot-roast with potatoes and green beans and homemade biscuits with real jam and butter.

I liked the food, but I also like the freedom to move and fresh air to breath when I am running at forty knots in the open bay waters of my own boat. This "pig-boat" was lucky to hit five knots under water, so it was going to be a long trip. Our PT boat was a simple instrument compared to having to operate a sub. No Thank You, keep me in the boats.

We pulled into the bay at midnight the next day, and a small boat met us a few minutes later to take us into the small make-shift base used by the two PT boats assigned there. I found cots for my men, and we bedded down for the rest of the night after putting aside the steak sandwiches that the sub's cook sent with us as a parting gift.

They had sent twenty-eight sandwiches with us since I told them the two crews that were here were roughing it on C-Rations that were airdropped by a passing bomber every two weeks, so we made sure to save the sandwiches for the morning to give to our new crewmates.

In the morning I woke up to find everyone eating a steak sandwich and laughing as if they had known each other for decades. This was the ice breaker I needed to get in good with the new crews.

I met my X.O. he was Ensign Ivan Ramos U.S.N.R. from Indiana, He had been a fullback on the Notre Dame Football Team and got the story about the incident that took the life of the skipper and the other men. They had been out for almost sixteen hours total on patrol and were about an hour away from base when a jap plane came out of nowhere and flew up their wake and strafed them without dropping a bomb, the Capt. and two other guys were killed instantly, if the plane had dropped a bomb, they all would have died.

Ramos missed getting hit in the attack because he was down in the galley getting another ham and cheese sandwich for him and the skipper. The third man that was hurt in the attack died early the next morning from his injuries.

The X.O. said that we could go to the boat at any time to check out my new boat, so I finished getting dressed. We had cut our long pants down to shorts a long time ago, and most men walked around in t-shirts and shorts, but today they all wore the normal work shirts until I could get used to who everyone was and their ranks.

My crew filled in where they were down, they had lost two Gunners-mate's and one Boatswain-mate, so we had an extra S1c Boatswain-mate, but that was ok, he was good, and he would fill in where needed, it would not be long until he would get a promotion to Chief and he would get transferred to new construction back in the states or to a boat that needed a chief.

We all could have taken a survivor leave for up to thirty days after having our boat sunk, but I still had a score to settle with a certain jap destroyer, and now I owed somebody twofold.

Besides, you never know where the Navy would send you when you come back from leave, I could have been sent to the Atlantic Ocean and had to fight German U-boats. No, I want to kill japs, japs, and more japs and that was in the Pacific Ocean, not the Atlantic.

General Douglas MacArthur planned to use The Navy Task Force under the command of Admiral "Wild Bull" Halsey and his Aircraft Carriers to bomb the islands up "The Slot" and to drive the japs from their new homes.

Our first mission was to be on lifeguard duty and be ready to save any pilots that had to ditch in the ocean after a bombing run to plaster the bases at Rabaul, so we were going to run up to the Bougainville area and find a place to hide out until we were needed. We ended up saving two crews the next day when they had to ditch due to damage the airplanes had suffered during their bombing runs.

None of the Pilots were injured so it all came out good after we got them on-board the PT boats and we were far enough away from Rabaul that the japs did not see where they came down. We got them back to our base and radioed for a sub to pick them up, one was coming our way in a week so they would have to relax and wait.

They wanted to get a sub returning from a patrol, not leaving on a new patrol, that could mean a two-month delay in getting the pilots home again because they would have to go out on patrol with them.

We went out two more times in the next week and saved a total of sixteen more bomber crew members, and they all knew each other, so the reunion turned into a welcome home party so now we had to let the sub know that they had a total of twenty passengers to pick up and we needed some extra food from them if they could spare some.

Our visitors did not like to stop eating after one helping, they were used to eating all they wanted on a carrier. The nice thing is that the carrier air wing commander was so happy that we had rescued his downed airmen that he got permission to make a special drop with a few “Ducks,” these were special purpose airplanes that had a float on it to let it land on the ocean and it had plenty of room to haul food and supplies for us that we could not get through our regular channels. These planes were able to land on the water and taxi right into our lagoon and up onto a beach, they had pontoons with wheels on them.

#17 US Navy Photo Courtesy of Flickr.com

Do you know how special ice cream can taste after NOT having any for almost two years? I did not believe them when they said that they had ice cream packed in dry ice for us along with cooked chicken breasts and cooked hamburgers and steaks with buns and condiments and all the trimmings.

Along with the food was a note from Admiral "Bull" Halsey himself, personally thanking us and saying that he was putting us all in for medals and he needed more courageous men like us that would go into harm's way to save pilots that had to ditch. He also said that there was a stand-down underway and that we would not be needed for at least a week so "Bon-appetite."

The food stayed frozen until we were ready for it since they had packed it in separate insulated tubs with dry ice. I think after we had all gotten over the Tijuana-two-step from eating such rich food we all gained at least ten pounds.

The Admiral was not going to be doing any flying close to us, but our local command had other ideas, they wanted us to land a ten-man team behind enemy lines on Rabaul and pick them up a week later so we had to put our picnic on standby until we could get back.

A sub could not get close enough to the island due to the outlying reefs and shoals, but we could get to within 100 yards and set them off in a rubber boat.

We would have to use both PT boats and break the ten-man team into two teams in case anything would happen, at least some of them could get there and map out the possible landing zones for a future amphibious landing that was in the planning stages.

We pulled up close to the sub and took on our passengers and stowed the rubber boats for use later that night. We made really good time on the run up to Rabaul figuring we would get close to the coast around 3 a.m. so that they could make the beach and our boat crews could return to the PT boats still in the dark. I had Ramos, my X.O. take one rubber-boat, and our chief led the second one.

We did not want to leave the rubber boats on the island in case they were found by the japs. This was just one less thing the Army Scouts needed to worry about hiding. The leader of the Scouts was a Capt. Baker, and he said, this should be a cakewalk, he had done the same thing on a dozen other islands. So, he would contact us with a flashing red light at 03:00 from the same area we were dropping them off at seven nights from now. We said our good-byes and our two-man boat crews made their way to shore to drop them off.

It took our guys longer to row into the shore due to the prevailing currents but they had help coming back out, so we were only a little behind our projected leaving time of 04:00, and the eastern horizon was starting to get light, sun-up was due at 05:00, so we needed to hustle out of the area so as not to arouse any suspicion.

We could not go full speed out of the area due to the rumble that our Packard engines would make, so we had to run at ½ speed with our mufflers on to dampen the sound from the engines, this actually sent the engine exhaust down into the water so you would not hear it. After thirty minutes we were finally able to lift the mufflers and go to full speed on all three engines.

We needed to find a hidey-hole to spend the day in hiding from any jap search planes that might come along. It was getting to light to be comfortable running when the enemy planes would be airborne on their morning patrols.

We found a small uninhabited island, and we tied up under some type of banyan tree that had extra-long leaves for the day. I posted a watch and told the rest of the men to take a nap and told the man on watch to call me in four hours.

In four hours, it was my turn at the watch, everyone else was fast asleep, so it was easy to listen for any noise that might be different than the normal jungle noises that we were hearing. You might not hear the enemy creeping up on you, but the monkeys in the trees would let you know something was not right by falling silent quickly at the first hint of trouble. Even the creepy-crawlers on the ground would stop making their chirping noises and come to a stop.

If anyone had been walking along in the jungle, we would have heard them using machetes to hack away the jungle growth as thick as it was. I got everyone up and told the cook to keep it simple for a light supper and water to drink and that we would leave after dusk. That would get us home around 01:00 and we could eat and sleep the next day away as long as the boats checked out ok.

We got in at 5 a.m. due to the other boat had an engine casualty that slowed us down to ½ speed, they would have to rebuild it instead of going to sleep. It would normally take them about eight hours to tear an engine down and replace the rings and maybe some pistons, but our motor-macs offered to help the other boat so it should go quicker.

We all ate some breakfast, and most of the crew stretched out on the deck or in hammocks stretched between a few trees to get some shade from the hot daytime sun. If there was not a war on, it would have been pretty out there like in the movies. I was warm enough that I woke up after a few hours and took a swim to cool off, then I checked in with the motor-macs to see how they were coming on the engines.

About another three hours and they would be ready to test the engines to see if the repairs would hold. I checked in with the radioman to see when he could send a message to the base that we dropped our passengers and were fixing an engine at this time. We also asked them to include some repair parts for the engines in the next supply drop, in case we lost another engine.

I also had him ask for a couple of .45 cal. Thompson Machine guns and extra ammo with spare magazines to be included in the drop for us to use, just in-case we had a close-up meeting with any japs. We usually only had 2/3 M-1 .30 cal. Carbines for personal use, now for some more sleep.

I had the radioman check in with HQ when we woke up, and we were given a priority-one message to decode that was sent to us. We had to run up to a small island called New Ireland that was part of the Admiralty Islands. It would be about a 200-mile trip.

There was an Australian Coast Watcher, that was given a heads up by some natives, he found out that there was a group of Americans that were stranded near New Ireland and needed to be rescued.

Now we usually did not provide a taxi service for people that were stranded because of a war that happened to break out. But there was a twist in this part, one of the ladies was the wife of an American Senator named Able.

She was on a trip to visit her brother, who was a missionary in the South Pacific Islands when the war broke out. They were trying to get back to Australia when their ship was sunk by a jap submarine, and they were able to get 10 people to a lifeboat and row to an island.

They had to leave that island after they found the island was inhabited by a large jap garrison, so they rowed to a smaller island that was uninhabited about a mile away and held out there, but their supplies were running out.

There were ten people in the group, six women, four men, and they were limited to the emergency food that was packed in the raft. Four of the women were nuns, and they were afraid that the japs had heard of where they might be hiding and were afraid that their days were numbered. I sent back a coded message that we would be ready to leave at dark.

We left just before dark in a rainstorm with heavy cloud cover, and there was no moon to show the enemy where we were going. With the cloud cover, there would be no night-flying bombers to contend with so we could relax a little bit during the trip. We would inflate the rubber rafts when we got to the island.

There were two PT boats going on the trip so we could divide up the number of people on each boat since adding another ten people to one boat would make for a tight fit. When we got to within about twenty miles to the island, we slowed down and went in with our mufflers on to hide the sound of the three Marine Packard engines.

We saw a few beach fires burning on a larger island, so we knew we had to give them a wide berth. Fires meant a jap garrison, and we did not want to wake them up. As we came around the island, we saw what looked like a small island with a channel about one mile wide between them. That had to be the island we needed.

Both of our boats coasted up to the island, but we had to stop about 100 yards out due to a reef, so the rubber boats would be inflated and would have to row a little further than planned. I had originally planned on floating our PT boats right up to a beach and taking on the people, but that idea went out the window with the reef.

The group of survivors was not at the beach as we were told they would be, so the boat teams were going to have to go looking for them. They set off in two different directions to save time. Ramos came upon them first on the opposite side of the island. One thing that we were not told was that Mrs. Able was pregnant, I mean very pregnant! And she was in labor.

The good news was that the nuns were trained as nurses so they could do all the hard things, the bad news was that they had none of the supplies they would have had if they were back on their original island. Ramos thought he heard a woman scream, thinking that they had been captured and were being tortured, he went running in with an M-1 rifle leveled and ready for action.

What he found was a lady laying on her back, with her legs bent up at an angle, and her dress pulled up way past her waist. There were two nuns in the baby receiving position and two nuns at the woman's head helping her to breathe. The men in the group had their backs to them and saw the sailors coming through the high grass at the last minute.

Once Ramos realized what was going on, he stopped in his tracks, and the other sailors ran into him. Mrs. Able let out a blood-curdling scream and the one nun told her to push through it, the baby was crowning. The baby came out in a splash along with a gush of blood and fluid. The nuns jumped into action to clean the baby's mouth and make sure it was breathing on its own. They wrapped it in one man's jacket and cleaned it off the best they could.

The first nun said that they needed to cut the umbilical cord, but they did not even have a knife, so one of the sailors had a Boatswain Knife on his belt, so they used it to cut the cord between the mother and the baby. The baby started to cry so they placed him on the mother's chest and showed her how to feed him. The sailors turned their backs out of respect for the mother.

I told Ramos to hurry when he went ashore, so we had as much time to clear the area as we needed. I did not know what was delaying him and I was getting worried. I did not know if I should send in another team or not when we saw activity on the beach. They were getting the boats in the water now so I could breathe a little easier.

I used the binoculars to take a look, and I saw Ramos carrying a package, I counted nine members of the rescued party, and my four guys, two of the sailors were carrying a homemade litter with someone on it.

I had no idea what was in the package or who was on the litter or why. We would figure that out when they got aboard, we have to make two trips to get everyone aboard the two PT boats safely. When the first rubber boat pulled up one of the sailors yelled out that it was a boy!

I yelled back, "What's a boy?" then he told us that they had delivered a baby boy, that is what delayed them. I told them to hurry up we needed all the time we could get to clear the area and just sink the rubber boats, we can always get new ones. They carried the new mommy and baby down to the cabin and put them to bed in my cabin to make her more comfortable.

It was close to 02:00 when we left the area, and we decided to go full out past the island where we had seen the beach fires before. We needed to make up time that was lost when they had to deliver the baby. The rainstorms kept the waves down to a minimum, so we had a smooth run for almost fifty miles.

They wanted us to try to make it to New Georgia, so we were going to head that way. We had to stop and refuel on the way to New Georgia, but we made it. There was an Army Air Corps C-47 airplane waiting with a Doctor and two nurses waiting for our passengers.

We even had a fighter escort flying cover for us. It's amazing what kind of pull having a senator on your side can come up with to save his wife.

We had to find our way back to our base without a fighter escort. But we made it ok. I wonder if we get a medal for delivering a baby during time of war? Maybe I could get a Seabee from the metal shop to design a plaque with a "stork" on it and give it to Ramos!

The crew spent the next four hours refueling the boat so that it would be ready for the next day or night boat trip that we would be sent out for.

Chapter 6 - Want to Play Cat and Mouse

One of our jobs during the war was to harass the enemy anytime we could, but yet, not to let them figure out we were based this close to their northern bases. Tonight was going to be one of those nights. It was like playing cat and mouse; only the cat was much bigger than us, and he liked to play for keeps.

We were notified around lunch time that a small group of jap ships would be running down the slot tonight and would be passing us around 22:00 hours.

They would be trying to take some of their soldiers off a few smaller islands that we had leaped frog over last month. This was a new concept in warfare for us, we would bypass a group of islands and raid another. This kept the japs off center because they never knew which island we were going to invade, and we did not have to waste the lives of any Marines to attack an island that was ready for us.

My X.O. Ivan Ramos had gotten promoted to Lt.(jg) and took over the second boat when its skipper had been promoted to LCDR, and moved up to headquarters. I told the crews to be ready by 19:00 to shove off so we could find an island to cover our approach before the ships came by. We would attack the last ship in the line and then make a run for it. I was assuming that other PT boats would be doing the same thing further down the line.

I found a small string of un-inhibited islands with about 1000 yards between them that we chose to hide on the leeward side, then as the ships started coming by, we could slip up and fire a few torpedoes into the stern of the closest ship.

Right about 22:30, we saw them coming, they were two abreast, and there was six of them in a column. I radioed the other peter-tare and told Ramos to take the left-hand one, and I would take the one on the right. I would call him when I was ready to fire.

We moved into position in their wakes hoping this would add some cover to our plan, at 500 yards I called the other boat and told them to let them go. We both fired two fish with a five-degree spread hoping that at least one fish would catch him even if he turned trying to evade the incoming fish in the middle.

The jap navy must have the same problem our navy had, with keeping a night watch-stander alert after a busy day. They never raised an alarm, and all the fish hit home about the same time. The ships started sinking before you could say "Hari-Kari."

The depth charges in the brackets at the rear of the ships exploded when the stern sunk to around fifty feet, this killed a large many of the enemy sailors in the water that were trying to swim away to escape their sinking vessels. I had no problem sending those japs to meet their ancestors.

I got to add a destroyer to the side of the Forecastle along with the cruiser and the twenty-three barges we had sunk since we came out to the war zone. I finally felt like I had paid Tojo back for killing my brother Mike and losing my first boat.

All the others we get from here on out are just extra credit from now on.

We had to run messages from one island to another, and they would sometimes load us down with mail also, it was not hard work, but the sailors would almost swamp the boat when they saw you pulling into the pier with fifty mailbags on the bow of your boat.

Ramos's boat and ours were working out very well as a team, but tomorrow night we needed to pick up our scouts that we had dropped on the island last week. We went back to our hideout after dropping off all the mail and fueled up, and I told everyone to double check the supplies we would need and to be ready to pull out at 19:00 again.

It can take four hours or more to fuel a boat up to 3000 gallons from fifty-five-gallon barrels by hand, so the crew knew what they had to do. They had to roll the barrels over to the boat and hook up the hand-crank pump that we had and pump every gallon into the two saddle tanks that each held 1500 gallons. We had put a long enough hose on it so you could fill both sides without having to hoist the barrels onboard the boats.

We got underway just before 19:00 so that we could be off the coast of the island at 03:00 again like the first time, I had my boat teams take the Thompson machine guns with them, so I split them up between the two boats just in case we ran into trouble picking up the Scouts.

If they had been found out, then we would not see the flashing red light like we had pre-planned and we would not row into the beach area. These guys were tough enough that they would never talk even if they were caught by the japs and tortured. They lived their motto, “Death Before Dishonor” to the end if need be.

We had to avoid a couple of small destroyer escorts on the way to our pick-up point, so every spare eye was on the lookout for possible trouble. We did not plan on fighting our way into the beach, it was going to be tough enough for the guys to row the rubber boats without having to shoot your way in and off of the beach.

We pulled our boats into within 150 yards of the beach after seeing the red lamp flash which was the agreed-upon code, and let the boats go with two -men armed with the Thompsons and extra ammo magazines in each boat.

Everything was running as planned when we started hearing gunfire from the beach. We were running into trouble, and now we were committed, with four men in the two rubber boats about fifty yards off the beach and the scouts trying to run for the boats in the surf and fire into the jungle behind them. We heard a large explosion back in the jungle a ways off, not sure what that was.

I told my machine gunners to fire into the jungle and not hit the scouts, so they laid down some suppressive fire for them. We even sent off a few 37 mm anti-tank rounds for extra measure and hit a machine gun nest. I counted eight guys instead of the original ten on the beach and in the water, so they ran into some trouble. When we get them back on-board, we can talk to them and find out what happened.

Our guys had to continue the fire support until we got them loaded, I yelled for them to ditch the rubber boats and not to worry about bringing them back on the PT boats.

We needed to leave now because the jap troops would have called for their own support and I did not want to meet up with any fast patrol craft with all the scouts onboard, the extra weight would slow us down and lately we were only able to get up to thirty knots instead of the forty to forty-five knots we knew our boats could do if they had newer engines.

We pulled out and headed to the North to throw off any chasers, we did not want them to know what way we were really going to go. They could probably figure out that we needed to run to the South-East, but we would head up the coast and then circle back on the north side of another island

Capt. Baker told me they were being followed by a jap patrol for the last few hours, so they had left two men as a rear guard to cover the rest of them as they got to the beach, they came under fire from the rear as the rest of the team went for the beach area. As a signal that they were being overpowered and were not going to make it back, they were to set off a portable land mine in the path of the attackers that they had set up. This would buy some extra time from the jap patrol that was after them.

The problem was that there was another jap patrol that was waiting for them by the path to the beach, they got into a firefight and with our help wiped out the second patrol of ten japs, but the rearguard never made it to the pick-up point, so that meant they were gone. The gunfire we heard when we got there was the second patrol opening up on our scouts and the fire support we provided, helped them to get away.

I saw a boat coming around the south side of the island, so it was time to forget the mufflers and kick it in the ass. They fired a few three-inch shells our way, but the distance was opening between us.

We cruised around, and I was sure this would throw the japs off the scent of where we were coming from and then headed south-east toward home, but the sky was starting to lighten, and that would mean air patrols would be looking for us. We made it to the same little island where we had stopped seven days before and stretched out our camouflage netting to cover the boats from the air.

It was a good thing that we had found cover because the enemy aircraft started buzzing around with-in an hour after we got set up. The net made us blend in with the trees as if we were a part of them. They came close a few times, but we kept still, and they never did find us. I congratulated the men for not getting trigger happy, if one plane got shot down, they would send more to look for him and then they would send a couple of ships.

We found out a few months ago that there was a huge bounty on any PT boat that could be sunk or captured and if it was captured the bounty on a PT Skipper was up to 100,000 yen which would make you a like a millionaire in Japan.

The japs wanted our technology, they wanted a PT boat really bad since they did not have anything that could keep up with our boats. If they could learn our secrets, they could change the tide of the war or prolong it another two years. I do not know if they could make an engine to compare with our three Packard Marine 1500 Hp. Engines, but we were not willing to chance it.

All our PT boat Chiefs and officers had standing orders to burn their boats if they were damaged beyond repair or if the enemy was getting close enough to possibly capture the boat. The Navy would forgive you for blowing up your boat to keep it out of the enemies' hands, but I know that they would crucify you if you lost your boat to the enemy. No questions asked.

Sometimes our boats would run aground in the middle of the night on an uncharted reef, and that happened many of times (since we were operating with charts from the 1800s that some friend of Christopher Columbus made when he was going around the world. Some of the charts had notations like "watch for three-mast schooner that ran aground the year of our Lord-1826") and that would pose a serious problem come daylight when the enemy planes would come a calling.

Our charts were so bad that some guys would ask their parents to mail them a copy of the "World Atlas" or "Time Magazine" if they had a map of the South Pacific in it.

Our Navy did not want to spend money in the 1930's mapping out the world's oceans just in-case we might ever go to war, but the japs had been mapping out all of these thousands of islands and lagoons for the last ten years or more. So, if we ever got the chance to board a jap boat before we sent it to the bottom of the ocean, we were instructed if possible, to try to capture any maps and codebooks we could find.

We all carried 100 feet of heavy-duty rope just in case another boat called you. If another boat called you on the radio, you knew that they had done everything in their power to get the boat loose again and they needed your help like right now. Because the last thing you wanted as a skipper of a PT boat was to let the other skippers in your squadron know that you were not the eagle eyes that you had been saying during the daily card games and you were fast-aground on some uncharted reef or shoal.

If we could not get to them in time, they would have to burn the boat and deep-six the radio gear and the code books and then make it to shore and hope we could pick them up before the japs made it to them.

We would also pull another boat to our base for repairs if the engines froze up or they had enough damage that they could not make it on their own power for some reason, but the boat was repairable. One time, I had to pull two boats at the same time, for an hour over to a repair tender because something had happened to their engines.

I instructed them that if we were attacked from the air, we would cast them off and that they were to burn their boats and we would try to come back and pick the crews up later. We tried not to keep score, but there were a few guys that were getting famous for running their boats up on a reef so we were trying to plan a special award to present to them if we could get it together.

I figured the best we could do was make a traveling plaque that we could add their name and boat number to it and keep it at the Base

Operations hut. Maybe the Sea-Bees could help us out on this special project also. They would build you anything you wanted for a box of chocolate bars, heck they built us an ice making building on Tulagi to say "Thank You" for helping to get their equipment to them without getting sunk.

One night we got a "May-Day" radio message from a PT boat that was damaged and had wounded onboard, they were going to beach themselves about fifty miles up the slot from us, and they needed to be rescued before the japs caught up with them. I got the crew around, and we took off right away to try to get to them. They had a jap fast attack destroyer after them, and the skipper and the exec were both among the wounded, so the quartermaster was trying to steer them even though he was also hurt.

They made it to the island and got everyone off to the beach so they could open the fuel tanks and set off a flare gun to start the fire that would destroy the boat. The fire would destroy the PT boat, but it would also alert the japs as to just where the crew had beached it so they would just follow the smoke to the fire and hopefully find a PT-Crew to take captive. Our job was to get there first if possible and beat the japs to the rescue.

We sent off a message for the crew to head to the opposite side of the island than the fire so that we could find them easier, I did not know if they got the message or not, but we would try that first.

It took us about an hour at full speed to get to the area, and we could see the pillar of smoke from ten miles out, so we cut around the north side of the islands since the fire was on a south-eastern beach, we could see the jap ship anchored near the beach. We spotted our crew on a sandy beach on the opposite side of the island, so we pulled up as close as we could, and they swam the rest of the way to us. We rigged a rope ladder over the side and had some men ready to go in after any guys that could not make it on their own. There were only eight men in the water, they told us the rest of the crew was dead so we could pull out now.

I had an idea that the fast destroyer was sitting off the beach looking for the crew, so we went hunting. You need a little worm to catch a big fish, and the burning PT boat was going to be our worm today. We rounded the island, and sure enough, the jap had stopped in the little cove and dropped anchor, just waiting for us to deliver a couple of torpedoes into her sides.

She must have sent a couple of rowboats into the beach because I could see them sitting there, the crew was chasing shadows through the jungle. They did not know that we had the crew safely on-board waiting for the "coup-de-grace" shot. I sent two fish into her sides, and we watched them both blow-up, and the ship capsized onto her port side in about 100 feet of water. Of course, the depth-charges in the ready racks on the stern blew up at the preset fifty feet depth taking more jap sailors to meet their ancestors.

I got a couple of really nice pictures that I told the sailors we had rescued that I would get them a copy of the photo for them to remember the crew that died did not die in vain.

It took about three hours for us to take the crew back to our headquarters island so they could get de-briefed and any medical care they needed, it is tough to lose both of your officers and other men that you had lived with, worked with, and fought the enemy of your country with. Now they would also have to add, died with them, it hurts, but that is part of war.

You grow so close to your brothers-in-arms, when you have been in combat together you grow closer than any civilian could ever imagine.

We took them to the base and turned them over to the medical personnel to help them out with any injuries. I went to the base operations shack and made a report to the Captain; the yeoman took it all down in notes and typed it up for my signature, he is not the quickest typist, but he got it done in under two hours this time.

I went over to the mess tent and had a big helping of "Shit-on-a-shingle" to eat, along with a big glass of "orange-flavored bug-juice" to wash it down. That chipped beef was pretty bad, but it hit the spot when you wanted something hot in your belly.

You grew tired of eating C-Rats or powered eggs and fried spam all the time, but then we were at war, and you had to make sacrifices somewhere. I guess our diet was the easy area to sacrifice as far as the Navy was concerned.

Chapter 7 - One Arrow if by Sea

We pulled out around 21:00 the next night to be safe since we had a bright moon and our wakes could be seen as an arrow at night by a jap bomber.

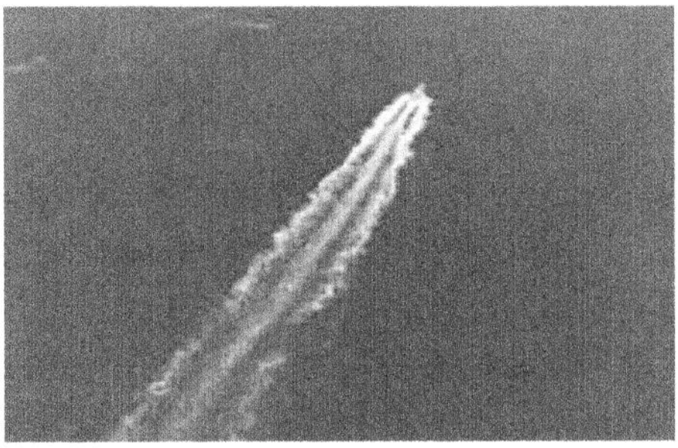

Photo #17A Courtesy of Wikipedia

The PT boats had the same problem with our wakes as the bigger ships had, only on a smaller scale, the green phosphoresce in the Algae actually glowed at night when it was disturbed by the screws of the passing ships. The japs could fly a bomber at night high enough that we might not hear him and then he flies right up our wake and drops a bomb right on top of us, our heads had to be on a 360-degree swivel all the time.

There were times when a boat would hear the bomber coming up his wake and then there were times that nobody on the PT boat was paying attention.

Sometimes we would run slow on two engines to keep the phosphoresce glow to a minimum, and if we detected an enemy plane, we would turn a 90-degree turn and crisscross our wakes back and forth a couple of times to confuse the pilots. Then we would engage the third engine and boogie out at high speed.

This tactic worked a number of times for us and saved our bacon but there were some boats that did not pay attention at night, and a lone bomber would fly right up the wake and plant a bomb right on the forecastle of the cabin causing an explosion that would blow that boat to splinters and usually kill all aboard.

I always had my guys with the best hearing and the best night vision stand the night watches so they could listen for any change in the sound of our engines which might indicate an airplane close to us. Sometimes just a different tone of the engine would end up being the sound of the plane's engine mixing with the sound of our engines, and that was enough to sound an alarm that could save the boat. We had that happen once when we were coming back from a long patrol, we never even heard the plane coming up our wake until the bomb exploded off our port quarter, it sprayed us all down like a summer downpour.

I held the wheel hard over to the left and yelled down for the motor-macs to gun the engines. I made a bunch of 180 degree turns to the left and right to confuse the pilot and any friends he might have with him. He flew off after one of our circles in the green colored algae of our wake looking for us.

After that scare, I told my crew that they would never get chewed out for a false alarm, but I would transfer them that day if they missed a plane coming in on us. And they believed me, we never had a sneak attack again because my guys were on their toes.

We got back to our base at 04:00 with this load of scouts and everyone went to sleep for the next four to six hours. I could tell that Capt. Baker was upset about losing his two men back on the island, so I told him that if he wanted to talk about it, I was a pretty good listener.

He felt like it was his fault that his guys got killed, they had been a team from the beginning and had gone through so much together, that they all felt that they would all make it home. He had made the same mistake we all did by telling his men that he would get them through this war.

Rule number one in a war is that young men die, and Rule number two is that there is nothing a leader can do to change rule number one. It is a shame that we have to lose a whole generation to stop some lunatic that wants to take over the world every thirty years.

Baker said that the two guys were some of his best silent trackers, they could do a sneak-and-peek even during the daylight and the enemy would never know they were even near the camp.

One time they even brought a samurai sword from the jap Commanders tent as a present for him to prove how close they had gotten. And they were the only guys that were fluent in the Japanese language, even with a California accent. They would be missed by everyone on the team.

The information they were able to get would save a lot of lives when the day came to invade that island, they were able to find four different landing areas and find out that there were a few different paths through the coral reefs that the landing craft could make it all the way up to the sand as if a bulldozer had plowed them a path 100 yards wide.

For some reason the coral did not grow as thick on one side of the island, I told him maybe it was because of that wicked current we ran into when we dropped them off. He agreed that could be it, but he was going to mention the fast current as a possible obstacle, so the landing boats did not drift too far off course.

They would have a submarine cruise by and take some pictures of the beach areas that they located, and they would do some depth soundings also so the planners would have an idea of what was waiting for them. Baker said that he did not have any idea when the invasion would happen but if it was like the other ones it would happen sometime in the next four to six months.

The Navy Planners had this Island hopping and invasion stuff down to a science now, there would be no more “SNAFU” like what happened at Tarawa where the Marines were trapped out in the bay at low tide, and the Higgin’s boats could NOT get across the coral reefs that surrounded the whole island.

Our Marines were made to wade in the surf for hundreds of yards, and it was like shooting fish in a barrel. So many good men were shot down in the water before they could even fire a shot. Now the planners would plan what day of the month to be able to use the high-tide water to help them get into the beach.

They would send in underwater demolition men the night before the invasion so that they could blow up any underwater obstacles that might stop the boats on their way into the beach. They also were making a new type of personnel carrier that had tracks on the bottom so it could climb over the coral.

Most of our transport ships still carried the boats with the ramp in the front until more of the crawlers became available, we had to share whatever new equipment came down the pipeline with the Navy landings in the Central Pacific that were going on at the same time. This helped to keep the japs off-balance so they could not build up their forces in one area.

We sent off a message that the package was picked up and we were told that a submarine would be by in forty hours to take them onboard. We were given a code that the sub was to use for us so we would not blow him out of the water. We were told to standby to assist the sub and not to plan on going out until they were gone. That meant we had almost two days to relax and get caught up on sleep.

Capt. Baker reminded me that everything I had just heard from him was top-secret and that I would be shot if I shared it with anybody. We went to breakfast and then to sleep. I let him use my hammock under the trees since he needed more sleep than I did.

I went down to the boats to see if Ramos needed anything for his boat. He was having trouble with his #3 engine so I told him he might want to have his motor-mac start on the rebuild, we were doing the same thing with our #1 engine. They were both low on pressure, and we could not be caught with our pants down at the wrong time. I let him know that we had forty hours before the sub was due.

I reminded the guys to keep one man armed with a rifle and to not leave the area and go wandering around in the jungle. They asked me if I was afraid of the boogie-man, I said no, but a crocodile can swim up undetected, and there are tigers that roam the islands, and I do not want to have to write your mommy and tell her that you were eaten for lunch by a tiger.

They caught on to what I was saying really quick. One of the Gunners-Mates loaded a rifle and stood by on the bow.

I had the Boatswain-Mate's take some scrapers and a dive mask and have a couple of the guys go over the side with them and try to scrape some of the growth off the bottom of the boat, it had been a while since we had them out of the water. This might increase our speed a little if they found a lot of growth.

I did not have to tell the rest of the crew to double check the guns, they were doing that as I was walking up to the boat and they already re-loaded the clips for the Thompsons just-in-case we had to use them again, they would be ready for action. I do not like to brag, but my guys were good!

Chapter 8 - Going up to Bougainville

We were told to take the packages to the sub and then continue back to our new base at the Island of Bougainville, they had set up a semi-permanent base with a couple of repair tenders set up to do everything we needed, and we were going to be given two weeks leave in Australia.

Our secret Hidey-hole was not needed anymore since we were moving up the Solomon ladder again. They were going to by-pass our island soon, but they would find us a new home.

Air travel was to be provided by The Army Air Corps, we were told to bring the best uniforms that we had, or we could get new ones in Fremantle at the Navy base. We were told that there was going to be a medal presentation with Admiral Halsey and Army General Douglas MacArthur present and we were told to be on our best behavior until after the ceremony was over.

We were going to get about four months back pay, and I do not think Fremantle would ever be the same again.

Ramos and I both were awarded the Navy Cross, and the Silver Cross with two Oak Leaf Clusters and all the men were given a collection of Silver Stars for the senior men and Bronze Stars for the Junior men. Ramos and I both also got promoted. He moved up to Full Lieutenant, and I was made a Lieutenant Commander.

I was afraid that they were going to take my boat from me since a Lieutenant was the highest rank that they would let you skipper a boat. I was right, but after talking to Admiral Halsey, he said that they had a new rule in effect now, that I would be in charge of four boats instead of just my own boat. I could choose to stay on the boat or run them from the shore and put another skipper on the boat. They were doing the same thing with Full Captains, they were calling them Commodore's and they would be in charge of four to six Destroyers. So, I was not going to be beached unless I wanted to be.

They put the officers up in a nice hotel that the Navy had leased for the duration of the war, and they had a private ranch about fifteen miles up the coast where the enlisted guys could eat, sleep, swim and even ride horses if they wanted to. The ranch invited us all to a home-made BBQ over a big pit in the ground. The beef was cooked for eight hours low and slow, just like the fancy places back home.

We even had all the beer we could drink, which was not bad considering that the stuff was being rationed in this country. They were saving all the beer they could make to send to the troops in different war zones around the world.

Both the countries of Australia and New Zealand had their troops fighting in North Africa and in Burma/India. They had to bring some of their troops home from fighting the Germans in North Africa in order to keep the japs from taking over New Guinea. Most of the men from the age of sixteen to thirty were overseas fighting, so the ratio of women to men was about fifty to one in these two countries, so you had your pick when you went out in town.

We always had a problem with the crew not wanting to take their Malaria pills every morning when we were in the South Pacific, someone had started a rumor that they would cause impotence, I did not hear anyone say they had any of "those" problems while on R&R.

We were not disappointed during our stay, a few of my men said they felt that they needed to get back to the war so they could relax and get some sleep.

I spent my time sleeping in every day and eating plenty of fruit and beef and potatoes, I had steak and eggs with fried potatoes for breakfast and a steak sandwich for lunch, I had to teach the cook how to properly fry up the french-fries real thick like. They made the best roast beef I had ever had for supper, then the leftovers were made into a beef stew. I never did learn to like "mutton or lamb" as meat, I was brought up on beef.

So, after two weeks of R&R, we said good-bye to the "Land Down Under" and flew first to Guadalcanal and changed planes before flying up to our new base at Bougainville. When we got to the new base, we found a couple of new Squadrons of PT boats and personnel and a surprise for both Ramos and me.

The repair tender decided that our boats had gone through more hours of use and refits than was recommended by the manufacturer and that The Elco Boat manufacturing Company actually wanted to take a boat apart that had been running strong for a year so they had shipped out six brand new boats with-out crews and shipped my boat back to the states so they could see where they could improve the next generation of boats.

They decided to retire Ramos's boat and use it for parts, so we were both getting brand new boats. The nice thing about this was that we would be able to do over forty-five knots again, which was not to bad considering that a normal enemy vessel would only be able to do about twenty-five knots on a good day.

We could actually run circles around any jap ship that decided to come down the slot. They had applied a special new paint on the hull to help keep the algae and the barnacles from growing to the surface, and the paint job above the water-line was done with jagged lines to make it harder for the enemy to see us and be able to judge our speed. Which might save us from a jap torpedo.

#18 Photo by NavSource-PT-170- Provided by Wikipedia

We were seeing this new paint job coming out on the newer ships that were coming from the states. The repair ships were starting to paint this new scheme on the boats that came in for repairs after they got the bottoms scraped in the floating dry-dock if they had one available to use at this base, they would spray paint them. Otherwise, they would lift them out of the water in a cradle and put them on the deck to do the work.

#19 US Navy Photo Provided by NAVSOURCE

We got to pick our weapon load-out for our boats, Ramos and I both wanted a 20 mm twin gun on the bow to use on aircraft and barges, and we both wanted an automatic loading 37 mm anti-tank gun mounted on the stern. All of our boats had started carrying the Thompson's for the crew to use for close in work, so we did away with the 50 cal. on the bow and added more of them along the sides.

We were changing from being a Motor Torpedo Boat to more of a Gun Boat. By swapping two torpedoes and the tubes for the two new guns, we were saving over 6,000 pounds of weight even with the extra ammo that we would have to store on-board. I decided that since these we would take a few days to break them in.

We also needed to add another crew-man to help with the ammo cans so that the guns could keep firing while they were reloading the ammo.

I now had an office on the base with my own Yeoman to help with the paperwork, I shared it with three other Commanders. I used to think that there was a lot of paper-work being a skipper of a boat, but now I was in charge of four boats, so that meant that the paperwork load just went up four times.

My first job was to get a new X.O. for my boat since my present X.O., Lt (jg). Smith was going to slip into the Skipper role. I told them to get underway and put about four hours on her in a slow mode and slowly add more speed until they were going full speed for at least four hours.

Then they would bring it back to the tender to make sure there were no problems with her. If anything needed attention, we had two mechanics that had come out with the boats from the factory.

I found an Ensign named Cameron that was without a boat assignment so, we did the paperwork and welcomed him to the Squadron, he would move into my boat as the next X.O. He was coming from a staff position in the States, and someone told him as a joke that he would need his dress whites and presentation sword for the dinner parties. It was kind of funny, to see a young college boy all decked out in his dress whites in the middle of the war in the Solomon Islands on his way to the mess tent. This comes under the heading of "Good Clean Fun."

I knew I had better nip it in the bud, or they would have him going up to the airstrip asking for a spare "spool of flight line," or they would assign him to the "mail buoy watch" on the mid-watch, so we did not miss the mailbag delivery that gets dropped off in a floatation bag at the marker buoy at the entrance to the bay by the C-47 from Australia. Those jokes might go over in the regular navy on a big ship, but we were more like a family here, and we did not need any bad feelings when it came to having to give or take orders during a gun battle.

Most times we never even salute an officer when we are out on patrol, or when we were on our little island. I did have to remind the guys that we were on a navy base and they needed to start dressing like sailors and rendering salutes to senior officers when appropriate.

We even had a few guys that looked more like well-trimmed Pirates instead of Sailors, so shaving kits and a trip to the barber were the order of the day. I told them that it was ok when we were living alone on a deserted island, but we were back in the Navy now. They cleaned up pretty good.

They had a few small leaks in the new boats that the company mechanics took care of. I asked Ramos how the boats ran? All he could say was "FAST" and walk away with a big smile on his face on his way to the mess tent.

I told Ramos that he was going to run an intercept that was starting to be used by other PT Squadrons along with the other three boats. The plan was to have a PT cruise along in an area that we knew there was going to be a jap destroyer or two on patrol. The other three boats would lay in wait and be ready to fire their torpedoes when the destroyers got into the trap.

I sent them to an area about an hour north of us to a group of islands we all knew. There had not been any enemy ships in that area for months. Ramos went out with the boats and slowed to a crawl when he got to the channel, they were going to use so that the other boats could site in on him as he came by.

All three of the other boats knew that he would be coming along in the next ten minutes, so they were ready for him. They were sitting at idle and taking it easy when they heard a PT boat go to full throttle, they were all like, hey what in the hell is Ramos doing? He was supposed to go by at ½ speed, about twenty knots but he must have been doing closer to thirty-five to forty knots.

Now they could see why he was moving so fast, there were two fast, jap destroyer escorts on his tail, and he was just now getting some distance when the three-inch cannons on the front of the ships opened fire on him, they were off centered of each other so they both could fire at the same time.

The main problem that our boats had at the time was that nobody had set up the torpedoes to be ready to fire since this was supposed to be a practice drill only. The three boats went in hot pursuit hoping to get a lucky shot "up-the-skirt" in other words right up their wakes. The Torpedo-men armed the fish quicker than they had ever done before in their lives.

All three boats fired at the same time with three fish, one on each outside and one down the middle of the two ships. The ship on the left could not go any further left because he was already too close to the island, so he chose to go to the right, and the guy on the right side decided to go left because he saw the torpedo on the outside of his wake.

The ships collided with each other and both were struck by the middle torpedo and they sunk within minutes of each other. Ramos came back along the track and pulled up asking what happened. After everyone quit laughing at him, they recounted what had happened after he pulled out ahead of the destroyers. He wondered why they did not fire right away, and now he knew.

I had a good laugh when they told me the story, but I told them, that is why we keep our fish ready at all times. You never know when the enemy might ruin your plans and open a door for you to get a kill. I split the kills between the three boats and told Ramos he did not get to share because he was the pigeon instead of the shooter. At least we know that the plan would work even if you had to adjust it a little bit.

We were going to start making patrols up the slot if the japs were going to start sending destroyers back down from Truk Island again. The naval base at Truk was one of the biggest around. They had a protected bay that could hold one hundred ships, and they had four airstrips on the island and over 100 bombers and fighters assigned there. It was reported that there were now over 100,000 jap soldiers assigned to the island.

If we had to invade that island it was going to be a blood bath.

I started having a team of PT boats go out every eight hours and run as far north-west as they could go, searching for any enemy war-ships and then come back a different way. By this time, we had air superiority in the lower half of the Solomon Islands and our area of control was growing by the week. We had the Navy Seabees building new airstrips as fast as we would take over a new island.

They would off-load their heavy equipment even as the Marines were still fighting for ground.

The Bees would use a crane mounted on a barge to scrape up corral to be spread out on the new runways, this would help to dredge a lagoon for bigger ships to be able to pull into a pier. They would load the corral onto a large dump-truck and run it over to the runway and dump it out there for the bulldozers and graders to spread out.

They had spreaders and rollers to pack the coral rock into what felt as hard as cement, and they would install this corrugated Marston-Mats for the planes to land on for the wet times during the monsoons

Photos #20-#21 US Navy Photo Courtesy of the WW2 Seabee Museum

They even set up large water pumps to spray salt-water from the lagoons to the corral to help it pack down. The marines would assign a rifleman to every piece of heavy equipment for the safety of the Sea-bees since there were still snipers on the islands even after they declared the island secured.

These guys were great, they could build you a small town out of the jungle and include an airport and post office too. They had salt-water desalination equipment to provide fresh-water for the occupants if there was not a fresh water source, and they even made ice plants to help cool the beer that came in by the cases for recreation. We were allowed two beers each day if you did not drink you could always find someone to buy your coupon and the prices went up like an auction whenever the temperature went over 120 degrees.

The huts that they built all had a shower area between them to share along with latrines, they even set up a laundry hut that could wash and iron officer clothing with a one-day turn around if needed.

#22 US Navy Photo Courtesy of WW2 National Museum

Chapter 9 - Going up the Slot

There were four different squadrons of boats based between the Tulagi and Tassafaronga and Guadalcanal area that helped to cover the south-eastern end of the Solomon's, they were being moved up to help us since the enemy had been either wiped out on each island or bypassed with no way to get food or supplies. They were going to wither away on the vine as General MacArthur had planned.

The Tokyo Express had slipped in and rescued as many japs as they could from Guadalcanal, which was being called "Starvation Island" by the enemy soldiers that were stationed there. The head of the Japanese Navy, Admiral Yamamoto actually had to fight to save these men because the General Staff in Tokyo had wanted to abandon them.

He explained to the Imperial General Staff that they could be saved and used to fight again in a final battle to save Japan. The soldiers were transferred to other bases and told to never talk about what happened under threat of death. The commanding officers committed suicide rather than have the loss of the battle, stain their family name.

We estimate that around 10,000 japs were saved from Guadalcanal, we would have preferred to have them die on that island instead of showing up ready to battle us again on a future island.

We decided to put a Squadron of PT boats on a few different islands to shorten the travel time from when we got an alert, to when we could attack the japs coming down the "Slot" We would have boats all the way from Guadalcanal going north-west up to Rabaul.

Our PT boats and our Submarines were the front line of attack for almost the whole first year of the war until we could build up another Navy. Too many ships were sunk at Pearl Harbor on December 7, and it would take some time for our steel companies to make enough steel for our shipbuilders to make more ships. We could make a new PT Boat in sixty hours, but it could take months to make a ship.

We would cover all the islands on the way to Truk that we had taken, the ones that were by-passed, we would continue to bomb and strafe any of the enemies that we caught out in the open, whether they were on an island or trying to get away in a canoe. We had airstrips on different islands so they could hit the enemy coming and going.

We found some barges trying to skim along from island to island, we were able to intercept most of them, but a few would get through. It is amazing that the japs would rather die for their emperor, who was a god-like entity to them than run away today to be able to fight again tomorrow.

When we would come upon a canoe, we would fire a few shots across the bow to get them to stop. If they had weapons and fired back at us, we would kill them all. If they put up their hands and wanted to surrender, we would take them, prisoner. The problem was that hardly any of them wanted to give themselves up because if you surrendered, you were already dead in their family's eyes, and they were afraid that we were going to treat them like they did to our men that were captured. I bet we only took on four or five enemy soldiers during our whole time in the Solomon Islands. It was just easier to shoot them then to take them, prisoners.

On the Island of Guadalcanal after our Marines had landed in August 1942. It was hard to find a US Marine that would take a jap prisoner after what they had done to the Marines that went up the beach to find the japs that "wanted to surrender" as the lone prisoner had stated. The japs not only butchered the Marines with bayonets after they had killed them on the beach, but they had also cut off their penis's and stuffed them down their throats after they had severed their heads with a sword. Our guys went back to avenge the deaths after they had found them.

Only two men escaped the carnage by swimming out away from the beach and diving down deeper than the bullets that were flying their way. They made their way back to the safety of the American lines and recounted what they had gone through. That is why the Americans did not want to take any prisoners if they had an option.

I assigned my four boats and had another four boats from another Division to go to the area of Kolomeangara to wait for a couple of enemy ships that were trying to evacuate some high ranking General and his staff, I told them to set up an ambush for when the ships had come to a stop to on-load their passengers. They were to be ready to shoot all of their tubes at the same time to make sure the ships sunk. I put Ramos in-charge of the attack. They split up and hid behind two different islands next to Kolomeangara and waited for the two destroyers to come slipping in with a rain squall that was moving in.

I made sure that two of the boats had this new thing called "radar" installed on them, it would paint a picture on the scope when a reflection of any metal was picked up by the receiver after sending out a type of radio wave. It would show distance and direction so that they could see on a dark night or even through the rain.

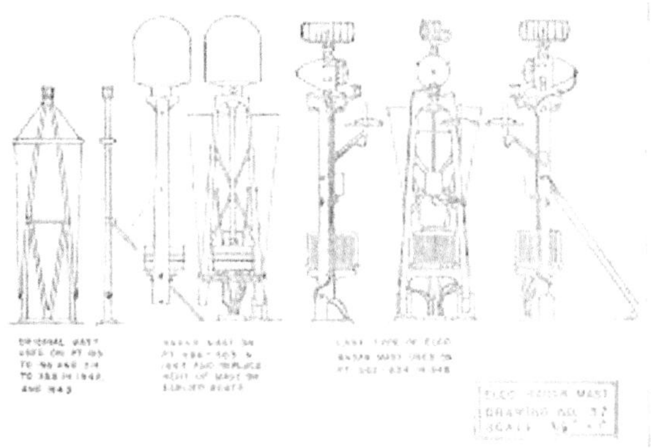

#23 Drawing from Elco Boat Company-1944 -- Provided by Wikipedia

Ramos saw the ships make their way around the island and come to a stop. They were ready to go on his signal of 1-whistle over the radio. They did not want to use words just-in-case the enemy was listening in on the radio frequency.

The code was set up as: one whistle to move into position, two whistles to get ready to fire, three whistles meant to fire at your target. God help him if he dropped his whistle overboard. They got into position using just one engine "mufflered" to hide the sound, they were all stopped and ready to fire at 1000 yards when Ramos gave the two whistles.

All the Torpedomen were ready for this shot. When the three whistles came, they all fired at the same time. There was a thirty-second-time frame for the run into the targets, and every torpedo hit its mark.

Both the new fast destroyers blew up just as they were getting ready to get underway. The heat wave from the explosion scorched the paint on the PT boats that were 1000 yards from the ships. Our crews even had flash burns on their faces. We think that the ships were carrying ammo and bombs to be dropped off at another island. This added bonus just made sure that the General was not going to keep his dinner appointment with the Imperial General Staff in Tokyo.

One benefit from being at the Base Operations was that I could write up the boats for medals that they deserved and walk them up to the Base Commander to make sure they got to the right people, up the chain of command. It was amazing just how many medals got downgraded because someone did not like that "they" did not have any medals to show off when they finally got to go home.

I met a Cmdr. that was jealous like that, he would downgrade a Navy Cross for a man that deserved it, down to a Bronze Star because he was a pencil pusher and he would never get a chance to win an award like that. I bet he got his Purple Heart from a paper-cut in Boot Camp, and he probably put himself in for it and approved it under a fake superior's name. I was hoping he would get his transfer back to the states, but without seeing combat, he would be waiting till WW3 to earn enough points to rotate back. I had problems like that every time I went to see him, to get a signature on a commendation letter or any award.

I got the Navy Cross for the skippers of the eight boats, and then I got Silver Stars for the Senior Torpedomen and a Bronze Star for the Junior Torpedomen with Unit Citations for all eight boats for their part of the plan. My Base Commander put me in for a "Medal of Honor" for planning this operation and for training the skippers, but it was downgraded by you know who to a Navy Cross. The loss of that jap General and his staff set the war effort back six months if it set it back a day.

I told Ramos that he had been approved for a medal for leading that operation at Kolomeangara and NOT dropping his whistle over-board. He smiled and said that his wife would enjoy the news. I said "WIFE"!! I did not know you were married! He said yes, him and his wife, Chelsea had gotten hitched at the "Justice of the Peace" the day before he shipped out.

He had gotten a week leave after graduating from the PT School at Melville before he had to meet his boat at New Orleans, so it was a quick wedding and then three days on a train heading south to New Orleans. He made it with three hours to spare.

Ramos said that he would write her the good news in the morning so it could go out in the daily mail run. I told him to get the men some chow and sleep because they were going to go barge hunting in the morning. He said they would make sure the tanks were topped off since he never knew how far I was going to send them.

I had the boats start making sweeps further out to see what they could find, they never found any enemy ships, but they were chasing a few different barges each night. The barges would head for shore whenever they sighted a PT coming at them.

Pretty soon the skippers came to me and said that the crews were getting restless for some action again, so I sent them out the next two nights. They had to go 200 miles out, and they only found two barges over the next two days. I told the Base Ops Cmdr. that I think the barges are drying up around here. He asked me if I was interested in moving up the "Ladder of the Slot" or did I want to stay around a little more? I just smiled!

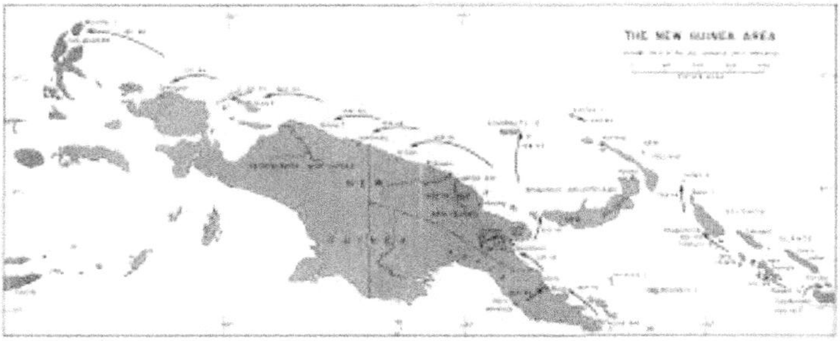

#24 US Army Map Courtesy of Wikipedia

Chapter 10 - Working for the Army now

Up the "Ladder," we were being sent up to Cape Gloucester to help stop the tide of barges running through the islands after General MacArthur's men island-hopped over them. Admiral "Bull" Halsey recommended myself and my boats to the General as a way to help stop the flow behind the American lines from getting out of hand.

If I had known that I was requested by a three-star Admiral, I might have put up a little more of a fight. The last thing I wanted was to be thought of as "easy," cheap, yes! but not easy. I mean hey, I could have held out for an extra $50 per month, but we were already getting combat pay with our sea pay, so that made a whopping $350. per month when a normal sailor was getting $75. plus, free room and board.

The US Army was making the trip up the "back of the Guinea Bird" They were hopping up the coast and by-passing some groups of enemy soldiers that were left behind "to wither on the vine" as Gen. MacArthur put it. But the Japanese Imperial General Staff wanted to save as many soldiers now as they could, so they were sending armored barges to rescue them.

We would go Barge hunting as soon as it got dark enough, they refused to run during the daylight because our fighter planes would tear them up. If we could find them beached during the day our Corsairs and the Avengers from the local airstrips could blow them out of the water.

They usually did a pretty good job of camouflage, or they hid up a stream where our PT boats could not see them during the day. One time we knew there was a jap base on this one island, but we could never figure out a way to find them. The barges were going up this stream, and they were covered by the tree branches all the way upstream.

We had really good information from some natives that were "hired" to clean out the trees from this area and build some huts about a mile upstream that the japs were using this hidden base as a staging area to send ammunition and bombs and soldiers behind the American lines to sabotage our aircraft and even our airfields.

We needed some way to get up-stream with-out being found out. Ramos came up with a plan that just might work. He suggested that we use three PT boats on a dark night and to back up the river as if we were barges! We could have a squad of soldiers go along with us, and they would walk on the sides of the bank ahead of us to take out any sentry's we might find. The soldiers would take out any sentry's quiet like so as not to arouse suspicion with the base soldiers.

I went to the Base Ops with his idea, and they loved it, but we would send four PT Boats instead of three. The added firepower would be helpful in over-powering the japs.

First, we had to add some portable side panels to attach to the boats to hide our normal equipment, the torpedo tubes, and the depth-charges were the biggest, but it would not be hard to hide them. The idea was to run in reverse at slow speed as if we were a barge and then when we got to the base area, we would open fire with everything we had.

I suggested that we use the Army Scouts team that we had dropped off at that island before. I found out that Capt. Scott and his team were on a neighboring island and could meet up with us in two days. That would give us enough time to get our supplies ready, find another two boats and also find enough jap uniforms for the crew of the first PT boat.

My crew dressed up in captured jap uniforms the best they could, it was hard to find the right sizes since the japs are smaller than our sailors for the most part. The hats and helmets and some of the shirts fit. The rest of the crew would wear dark green dyed t-shirts and hide in the gun tubs or in the cabin ready to climb up when we were in a position to open fire.

My Chief Boatswain Mate was a bear of a guy, and I told him it was his luck they did not draft a Sumo wrestler, or we would have had a uniform to fit him, He said that was fine, he would hide under the Lazarette with a BAR rifle and be ready to fire when I gave the go ahead. The guys were looking forward to a little fight now and then.

They were starting to feel like they were not really fighting the war or making a good contribution since they were only hunting barges, we had not fired a torpedo in almost six months, and they were getting restless.

We left the next night around 21:00 and went around the back way of the island and waited till the moon went down at 03:00. We dressed up as japs and pulled the boats in-river going backward.

The Scouts were sneaking up the pathway on either side of the river, I am so glad that the japs made a walkway.

They found a couple of machine gun nests and were able to dispose of them without even a sound. The jap sentries just waved us through thinking we were bringing them some sake wine with their supplies. But they would get a bigger blast in about sixty seconds. We pulled up to the dock, and I had the crew man their gun stations.

The Scouts started it off with a 40 mm mortar barrage on the huts of the village, and our 37mm anti-tank guns took care of two armored barges that were tied up ahead of us. The anti-aircraft guns were put to use tearing the scores of jap soldiers up that were running for cover. The Chief opened up with his BAR gun at a machine gun nest that they were able to man, the bullets tore them in half. A couple of our sailors got hit by shrapnel from the bullets before the BAR took them out.

We stopped firing to give the Scouts time to run through the base and find the ammo stash. It was about 100 feet beyond the camp perimeter to the north, so they set some bombs on a timer and set the camp to blow in five minutes, I told them it would give us enough time to clear out and get down river far enough to avoid the blast.

Capt. Baker set the timers up while the teams were loading onto the boats, when he came running, we were ready to move out and did we ever. The first boat made it to the edge of the river bank and the ocean when the blast tore through the jungle, we could hear shrapnel whistle through the trees above us.

We took off as fast as we could when we cleared the mouth of the river and raced back to behind the American lines. We checked in with the Army base when we dropped off the Scouts, but we kept some of the extra guns for good measure. You never know when a mortar tube and twenty-four rounds might come in handy.

I talked Capt. Baker into getting me some more cases of mortar rounds so we could go out to sea and practice a little on a float that we would set out off the stern of the boat. If we could not hit it with the mortar rounds, then I would turn the boat around and let the 37 mm anti-tank gun do it. My Gunners-mates were crack shots with the mortar tube, and they had never shot one before. GM-1st Evans said that you just had to visualize where the round would land and adjust your angle from your first shot.

I wanted to try the mortar rounds out the next time we came upon a barge so we stored it in a rack on the aft of the radio-mast with six rounds in a ready-ammo can. We went out the next night and caught two barges skirting around an island, they took off for the beach when they heard our engines. They pulled into the beach and made a run for it into the jungle, there must have been fifty soldiers in each of the barges, so we peppered them with machine gun fire to keep them running while we set up the tripod for the mortar tube, it only took four shots to totally destroy both barges with the 40mm mortar, I could not wait to share my invention with other PT-skippers.

We had armed each of my boats with a 40 mm mortar tube, and they would fire a few shells at the fleeing barges. One time one of my new skippers had ordered his men to open fire with the mortar rounds, but just as they fired the first shell, he put the boat into a skid to the left, and they came to within twenty feet of taking a round on the chin. I had to explain to him that the mortar was more effective if it hit the enemy barge and not your own boat.

I got some extra ammo and had all of my boats go out and hit a sled that was being towed by another PT boat for practice over the next week. The other Commodores watched what I was doing and asked me to teach their guys how to use the 40 mm mortar too. We had to request twelve new Mortar tube set-ups through the supply system, but the Navy said that they were not allowed on our material sheets for a PT boat. I just had to find a supply Sargent in the Army that could help me out.

We got our 40 mm tubes and extra ammo for each boat, it is funny how the Navy can say that they are not allowed on a PT boat, but the Army had them coming out of their ears and could not wait to ship out a load to the Army Supply clerk on the base. I just had to find a whole lot of candy bars to fill the sugar need of these guys. My mom was my major supplier when it came to candy bars, I just told her that the guys were homesick for them and she would mail boxes out to me.

We ran around this area for two months cleaning out the enemy barges that were trying to run by night between the islands.

I was told to put the boats in at the PT-Tender/repair ship, and they would check them out while we were all flown to Australia for R&R again. When we got to Freemantle, they made a big thing out of what we did and had another awards ceremony and party. This time though they gave us new orders.

After debriefing with Army Intelligence and telling them how to go after the barges with a few ideas Ramos and I had come up with, they informed me that Ivan and I were being sent back to the states, and we would have thirty-days leave before reporting to Melville, R.I. as a combat-trained instructor at the PT-School.

Chapter 11 - Instructor at Melville

Our crews were being broken up and sent to new boats under construction. A few of the senior men would be instructors with us at the school to make use of our war experiences to teach future PT-crews to take the war to the enemy.

This new assignment was to last between twelve to twenty-four months at Melville. The US Navy liked to rotate its senior personnel back to use their experiences at war to help the new guys to know how to better fight the enemy, unlike the japs that worked the senior guys to death and then there was nobody to train the new guys.

Ivan and I flew out to Sidney to catch a Navy Catalina flying boat for a hop to Fiji and then America Samoa and on to Pearl. These airplanes were not made for a lot of comfort, that is for sure, but it was a lot faster than spending three weeks on a freighter, and it was way more comfortable than flying in a regular C-47 Army Transport.

I did not know until we got on-board the Catalina that it was actually Admiral Halsey's personal plane and that we were the only passengers, talk about plush.

They had a full bar and staff, and the boxed meals were not your normal box meal that we would have gotten on an Army transport, and even the blankets and pillows had three stars embroidered on it.

We spent the night at Pearl Harbor in the visiting Bachelor Officers Quarters (B.O.Q.) and were told that we had to meet with Admiral Nimitz at his office at 07:00 for breakfast, and that a driver would be here at 06:30 to pick us up.

We had a packet of things that Admiral Halsey had sent with us with explicit instructions that we were to hand these to Admiral Nimitz, I thought he was joking, but the packet had an official wax seal on it so they would know if we had opened it.

I did not like going back to the states when the war was going better for us now, I would rather be on a PT boat riding the waves and chasing jap ships.

We were ushered into the dining room when we got to 10 Makalapa, which was Nimitz's headquarters and the support buildings that were built into a mountain above the submarine piers, and it had the housing and offices for the Fleet Adm. and Pacific-Commander-in-chief.

#25 US Navy Photo- NAVSOURCE by Wikipedia

The Admiral always woke up around 05:00 and went for an early swim before breakfast, so he was already working on paperwork when we arrived at 06:45.

He motioned for us to get a plate from the buffet cart and to sit down and help ourselves to breakfast and he would be with us after he looked through the packet that we had brought in with us.

Ivan and I both took fresh fruit and scrambled eggs with crispy-country bacon. The Admiral even had his fresh strawberry preserves that his wife sent him for the biscuits. The admiral's bright blue eyes could bore right through you.

#26 US Navy Photo-Provided by Wikipedia

The Admiral finished his plate of fruit and eggs, and the wait staff poured us cups of coffee and left the room. Now he said, thank you for bringing him the updated info from the S.W. Pacific Commander and for making sure it did not get opened. He wanted to know if we wanted to know just what we brought with us?

Ivan and I both looked at each other and said, "if you want to share it, sir." He said that the packet had some photos of some Jap held islands and a new plan to invade the islands when we were ready. He said it also has a personal note from Admiral

Halsey about my two couriers eating my biscuits and jam.

I almost choked on my coffee and my third biscuit! The Admiral chuckled at my discomfort. He read the following note from Admiral Halsey;

Dear Chester, these two Officers are going to be sent to Melville, R.I. to become instructors at the PT-School, I understand the need for our combat-tested seniors to help pass on their knowledge to the new officers that are coming up the ranks, but I wanted to ask you to intervene with this one. I believe that the war effort would be better served if they went to Melville for sixty days to be able to talk to two different classes and then send them back to me for reassignment. I have a need for two high caliber officers like them to head our PT-Program in the SO-WEST-PAC area in the coming months.

In order to assist me with the British could you promote them, so they have a little more clout. I need Beck to be a full Captain and Ramos to be his assistant at a full Commander, the British Commander here is acting uppity toward my new Commander, and this would help to smooth some ruffled feathers when we go to another Allied meeting. Let me know what you think. With my warmest, Bull.

There was total silence in the room. Finally, the Admiral said, "I concur with Admiral Halsey's recommendation, what do you guys think? feel free to speak".

I said I could not believe what I was hearing, and Ivan said are you sure he means us? The Admiral said, "Yes Commander Ramos, he is talking about you." He said that he would send a message to Admiral King in Washington and the Chief of Naval Personnel to let them know to advance you both two pay-grades effective today and to change your orders. He also congratulated us on the awards that we earned in the last twelve months and said they were well deserved.

He told us that, "You will report to Melville in two weeks to catch the last month of the present class of students and then stay on for the first month of the next class. Then you will report back here to see me before you leave for Australia. Congratulations Gentlemen and good day."

We stood and saluted him and was shown to the door by an aid. When we got outside, I told Ivan, see how smart that aid was, you need to learn how to do that stuff for me. He just laughed, but he did open the door to the sedan that was waiting for us.

The driver took us back to the B.O.Q. at Pearl and he said that he would be available to drive us anywhere we needed to go, he was instructed to stay by us until we flew out the next morning. He also had new collar devices for us that Admiral Nimitz had said to give to us. So now we did not have to go to the Base P.X. to buy them.

I suggested that we go to the Officers Club and celebrate so Ivan said, Yes Sir as you wish. We ate an early lunch and shared a few drinks then we both rode over to Western Union and sent a telegram to our families that we would be home in a few days and that we would update them at that time.

Ivan would go home to Nappanee, Indiana to see his wife and I would go home to South Bend,

Indiana to see my folks and mourn the loss of my brother. We would fly to Chicago together and then fly into South Bend Field, and our families would pick us up from there. We went to bed early since our Navy flight would leave at 04:00 for Long Beach.

The flight to Long Beach was fine, but our flight across country, was a challenge, you would think that being in the Navy would give us front of the line privilege, the trouble was that there were hundreds of service personnel making flights coming and going and "rank has its privilege" was the thing you heard the most.

We got to Chicago and found another Captain on our flight that had a Navy car taking him to the South Bend area, so he offered us a ride. Capt. Thomas was on thirty days "survivor leave" from having his destroyer shot out from under him. On the trip from Chicago, he related to us how his ship sunk.

They were on a three-destroyer patrol about 150 miles from the Admiralty Islands one night searching for a cruiser that had been missing for the last couple of days. They saw an oil slick on the water and then started seeing some life-boats tied together with other rafts. They stopped in the middle of the rafts while the two destroyers kept station around them.

It was never a good thing to come to a full stop when you found survivors in the water because the submarine that sunk them might be playing possum under the waves just waiting on another sucker to take the bait. They thought they would be fine with the extra destroyers, but after about five minutes a torpedo came out of the north-west and blew the bow of his destroyer right off his ship.

They had to abandon ship while the two destroyers gave chase on the sub, they were able to bracket him with depth-charges, and then one exploded under him and split him in half. They actually saw both ends come to the surface before they sunk into the depths of the ocean.

They only lost forty-seven guys on his ship from the crew in the attack and fifteen guys from the lifeboats were also killed. The rest of both crews were picked up by the other two destroyers and brought back to their base. They were loaded down with survivors that were all covered with bunker-fuel oil that they swam through. The corpsman used gasoline and kerosene to wipe the oil off the skin the best they could. Once cleaned, they could see and treat the injuries.

The Capt. came out with a broken arm from when he was bounced off the side of the wheelhouse when the torpedo exploded. Now he would go home for a month and then go back to Pearl for reassignment.

We told him about our story, and he was amazed that we had rubbed elbows with Admiral's Nimitz and Halsey and even the "General of the Army"- Douglas MacArthur. He said that he had seen Nimitz once from a way-away. He was being driven over to the Submarine base to welcome Mush Morton back from a great patrol and to award some medals to him and the crew of his Submarine.

One thing about Nimitz was that he really cared for his sailor's well-being, he rented the Pink colored Sheraton Hotel on Waikiki beach for the duration of the war. It was located right next to the Army's "Fort Derussy" This was used for the R&R of the submariners when they came in from patrol. Any extra rooms were allocated to any Naval Officers and then senior enlisted as room would allow.

Admiral Nimitz remembered all the names of the officers he had met and called you by name the next time he saw you. His memory and recall were outstanding, now that was both good and bad.

If you had gotten on the Admiral's bad side, he would not be-rate you in-front of anybody else, but those deep blue eyes would burn a hole in you and let you know that you had just messed up in front of the Pacific-commander-in-chief. He would have an aid speak to you later, I was glad that we were in his good grace at this time in our lives.

They dropped us off at the South Bend airfield since that was where our families knew we were coming into, but we were about two hours ahead of schedule, so Ivan and I went to the snack shack next to the terminal area and got a sandwich

Ivan's wife, Chelsea, got there first so I told him to meet me in Melville on the first of the month and they took off in her dad's car that she had borrowed for the trip. My dad showed up about thirty minutes later driving a 1940 Studebaker sedan, he loved his Studebakers and took really good care of them. He used to work at the plant in South Bend that makes them, now they were making large trucks for the military. Nobody was making cars at this time, everything was geared up to make everything that we needed to win the war effort.

It was nice to get home again, but I had been around the world, and now I knew that it was not flat. I grew restless just sitting around, relatives kept coming and going asking me about the war. I figured out the best way to shut them up was to say that the information was secret, and I could not share it. You know the old saying, "Loose Lips-Sink Ships" so I kept my mouth shut. If I had told them the ugly truth about seeing men shot or burned alive in a fire on the water, they would have never closed their eyes at night again.

My dad just put his hand on my shoulder one time after dinner with relatives and said quietly to me, "I am proud of what you have become, always do your best, and you will never hang your head in shame." My dad was wise beyond his years, he went through WW1 and never talked about it to anyone, he spent three years on an old destroyer in the Atlantic Ocean as a Boatswain Mate, so we had something to bond with now. Ah, but he was not a "shellback," so I was one up on him now.

It was harder to say good-bye to mom this time seeing how Mike was not coming back. My little brother was still too young to join up, and I hoped that the war would be over before he got of age. I wanted to get back to killing japs, but I could not say that to the family, they might not understand.

I made it to the PT-school one day early to give me time to check in and get situated, Ivan was already there and had the information we needed on when and where we would speak to the students. We were going to split up so that we could have a little more personal time with ½ of the normal sized classes instead of putting them all in one gymnasium and putting them to sleep by talking for the whole time.

I allowed questions in my classes, and some of them were pretty well thought out ahead of time. We even took our chow time with them to let them know that we were just like them.

They were asking pointed questions about the handling of the PT boats and any problems we were having with them. I was told that a large number of the items I pointed out about our first boats had been corrected with the new generation of boats that were being delivered now.

I guess it really did help to send my original boat back to the builders. I told the students about us becoming more of a gunship so not to put as much energy into the torpedo sections of the Curriculum, I got some sour looks from the regular instructors, so I told them I was just joking about not studying about the torpedoes.

We got to spend some time with the other instructors in the evenings, it was fun to compare notes on where we all served. I met one skipper that had served six months in the Bering Sea around Alaska. His biggest complaint was the lack of heating for the crew quarters of the PT boats. I was glad I served in the South Pacific and not the Northern Pacific.

Our time passed quickly at Melville. It was different to be able to eat regular food all the time, we were not looking forward to C-rats and rice or canned spam with beans and old bread.

Ivan and I flew out at the end of the month and reported to Pearl Harbor so that we could pay our respects to Admiral Nimitz. He was a busy guy, but he greeted us as if we had been old friends. Like I said earlier, he remembered our names and even asked about our families back home.

He asked us what we thought about the newest class of PT-Officers we had met at Melville? I told him that they were top notch and would do good where-ever they served. He said that was good because we were going to need them, we have been getting hit pretty hard when it comes to PT boats in the SW-Pacific. We had lost about twenty different boats and crews in the last two months all around the Solomon's.

I told him I was looking forward to getting back to the business at hand. He said that we would be flying back in the morning to Australia to meet up with Admiral Halsey and that he sent his plane to pick us up.

He bade us farewell, and we checked into the B.O.Q. for the night. At 05:00 we had our wake-up call so we could get to the air terminal for our Catalina. We flew first to Fiji to refuel and then on to Australia. It would be nice to be a three-star admiral and have your own flying boat, I could get used to this life.

The pilot let us take turns in the cockpit sitting in the co-pilots seat and getting able to handle the controls, I told him there was one big difference between flying a boat like this and piloting a PT boat, he said, "What was that?"

I told him that if he made a mistake, everyone was going to die, but if I made a mistake, everyone would just get wet and go for a swim at the worse. He laughed and said that was why they had to have so many hours in each type of airplane they were qualified to fly. He had thousands of flight time hours and was the top pilot in his last class, that is why he was picked to be Halsey's personal pilot.

Chapter 12 - Working for Bull Halsey

There was a car in the airfield to take us to Halsey's headquarters. He greeted us and explained to me just what I would be doing for him. There were going to be a lot of meetings and planning sessions, and Ivan would be a runner and assistant for me.

After we set up a plan, Ivan would get copies made and take them around to the different commands that were going to be a part of the plan and explain all the timelines to them.

Just like Nimitz had said to us in Pearl, we had lost a lot of boats in the last two months, so Halsey wanted me to look into all the incidents and see if there was any connection. Was there any way that the japs were reading our messages to and from the PT-Bases or was there a jap-sympathizer in the headquarters staff that was sharing the information with a spy?

I joined the Navy to be an Officer on a PT boat, and now I was being used as an investigator. I had Ivan run a background check on everybody on the HQ staff, we would start there and see where that took us.

I got to meet my British counter-part and Halsey was correct, he acted rather uppity to us the whole time we were in the meeting, he acted like it was beneath him to sit down with us. I told the Admiral that it might be easier to have him replaced. So, Halsey got with General MacArthur and made it happen. His replacement was a Major

Lee with the British Army. He last served in London on the General Staff.

We had done all the background checks and found two interesting people that I had questions about. One of them, a Major that had served in the Philippines for twenty years and another one that had served as an attaché with the Naval Commander who served in Russia.

We found out that the Major from the Philippines was ok after doing some more checking, but we were still going to rotate him out to be safe. He would go back to the states to an Army base in Texas.

The one that was the Naval Attaché to Russia named Franks was the top person on my short list so we would watch him carefully over the next few weeks to see what he did every day to establish a routine for him

I had Ivan follow him, he found out that the guy would go to a drycleaner's shop every Friday with a load of clothes and then he would return with his clean clothes in a package just like most officers did. The only difference was that on the days that we had a planning session he would make an extra trip to the cleaners.

I brought this information up to the Admiral, and Ivan suggested that we plan a fake session and see if the japs fall for it. Halsey said that if this is what it takes to expose a jap spy, he was all for it. We had info that the Russians might be in-bed with the japs and that they were sharing info back-channel behind our backs, somehow the japs were finding out our plans before we did them.

I planned for eight PT boats to make a night time run up to the island of Biak and to drop off a company of Scouts behind enemy lines, so we went through all the planning sessions and cut the orders, only these orders were not going to happen

We replaced the Biak Island drop-off point with the real one called Kavieng Island, and it was going to be two PT Boats and ten scouts. I had Ivan fly the actual orders out to the affected commands, and hand deliver them.

The spy would hand off his Biak plan, and it would be passed to the Russians and then passed on to the japs. We were not sure how the information was being sent out, but if it worked, we could bust a spy ring that was costing us a lot of good sailors. Ivan had the guy followed by a friend so he would not get suspicious if he saw Ivan again.

And once again this guy went to the cleaners on a mid-week lunch break with a load of clothes, boy this guy did not like to wear a uniform more than once.

The plan was to be pulled off in three weeks, so Admiral Halsey sent a message off to Nimitz at Pearl Harbor and had him get with his "Cryptologists" and watch for any jap radio traffic about sending destroyers to the Biak area on the night in question. It worked as planned, our radio detection units had picked up message traffic from Tokyo to their commands at Truk to send out a task force looking for eight PT Boats trying to drop off scouts behind their lines at Biak.

Admiral Halsey sent an American Carrier Task Force to the east of Bougainville to set a trap for the japs. We would surprise the japs when they were out looking for the PT boats that were not even going to be there.

Now to set up another trap, this time for the spy-ring. We wanted them caught red-handed with the plans. So, we had another planning session set up for the morning, this was going to be an "invasion" of Morotai Island by the Army.

Ivan had it set up with the Military Police to have twelve men ready to rush the cleaners to capture all the people involved. He told them to rush the back door at the same time as they went in the front so that nobody would get away.

Our planning session went from 08:00-12:00, and our pigeon was off to the cleaners an hour later. Franks was in such a hurry that he missed seeing an MP-jeep that was parked around the corner from the cleaners.

The Military Police raided the cleaners two minutes after he went in, they found the guy in a back office going over the plans with two men, one was the owner of the cleaners, and the other was talking with a Russian accent.

They arrested all of them and took them to the headquarters for questioning. The Russian was going to be handed over to the State Department for Deportation and return to Russia, but the Australian and the American were going to have a quick trial, and then both would be shot as a spy against America during time of war.

We found out that the Australian owner was a jap sympathizer and that he had been given a Russian from the Embassy as his handler to share info with Russia and then they would give the info to the jap attaché in Russia. So that was how the japs found out our plans and were able to intercept our PT boats on secret missions.

The secret trip to Kavieng Island went over without a hitch. Captain Baker and his scouts were at it again, and they pulled this one off just like other "peek and seeks." The info they sent back to us was first class, and they even had copies of where all the enemy installations were located and pictures to back it all up.

Capt. Baker had found out that I was on the planning staff so he sent an apology that they could not find an extra sword to send along with the info, maybe next time. I explained to Halsey that it was an inside joke.

I asked Ivan to find out where Baker's scouts were staying so we could send him some C-rats as a joke.

I was missing not being out on a PT boat, riding the waves and feeling the air rush past me doing forty knots but that was not going to happen anytime soon.

The Admiral congratulated us on sniffing out the spy-ring and told us that he was flying up to Pearl for a command meeting with Nimitz so he would be gone for a week. He told us about one time when he went to Rendova, he wanted to check in with the base commander and drop off some medals they had been waiting for.

While he was at Rendova they had an air-raid, and he had to run for a slit-trench, he hit the dirt, and a marine fell in on top of him. That marine started bitching about all of these stupid air-raids and how they were messing up his schedule, he wondered who in the world had ever picked this stupid island location? Halsey answered back, "I don't know, but if I ever find the "sum-bitch" I will kick him in the seat of his pants for you!" The marine climbed off and helped Halsey up and tried to stammer out an apology when he saw the stars on the collar, but Halsey stopped him and said, "I understand, son," and went on his way.

He said he hopes that never happens again, he tore his pants that day. We all got a good laugh out of that one.

If he was going to be gone for a week maybe, I could make a visit up the Solomon Islands and catch a ride on a PT boat again. I informed the Admiral of my plan to visit the PT-bases while he was gone and to check on the crews and the status of the boats and he said that sounded like a good idea.

I started out at Guadalcanal and moved my way north, hitting the different bases and making notes at every stop. Our Torpedo problems were getting solved, for the depth problem they applied a better seal that kept the salt-water out of the depth gauge. The water was corroding the tube to the depth mechanism, and it was allowing the torpedoes to run deeper than set.

And for the ones that would not explode when they hit a target, the manufacturer made a stronger hold-back pin that was sheared off when they hit instead of setting off the pre-fire charge that went off first, setting off the main charge.

The men were in pretty good spirits, and I told them that as we moved up the chain that more boats would be joining us, and conditions would be getting better.

I met a few men that were in the first class that I had spoken too at Melville and they said that I was not lying to them when I spoke about the living conditions out here. There were good days, and there were bad days, but over-all it was slowly getting better.

I got to take a ride from base to base on different PT's, and it was great. I ran into Capt. Baker and his Scouts on one island two days later. I gave him a box of C-rats, and he laughed and said he would share them with his guys.

He was supposed to go the next day ashore on another island, and he wanted to know if I wanted to go along on the venture, that way I would have the info Halsey needed right away when they got back in twenty-four hours.

It was set up as a simple "sneak and peek" on an island that had 100 soldiers max on it. We were by-passing another island that had 10,000 Army soldiers in their garrison that they had reinforced, thinking we were going to attack that island first.

General MacArthur's plan on island hopping was actually working, they were not sure what island we would attack next, so we were making them split up the available manpower and so the island we did invade had fewer men to man the installations they had built over the last ten years.

Japan had been given a large number of islands after WW1 that used to be controlled by the Germans and they were building up the defensive capability of them all. They would not allow outsiders around the islands, so the U.S. did not know what they had for defenses. Couple this along with our poor quality of charts and maps meant that we were at a big disadvantage when it came to navigating around all of these islands.

There were hundreds of un-charted coral reefs and shoals that could be very dangerous to our PT boats, and we needed to find out where they were before any invasion could take place.

There were two boats that were going to take the scouts to the island, and I decided to ride on the lead boat with Baker. I was only going along for the ride, but it was going to change really quick.

When we got to within 500 yards of the island we came to a sudden stop, this was so fast of a stop that everyone was thrown off their feet. We had run-aground on an uncharted reef!

Capt. Baker was knocked out, and three of his men were badly hurt. The skipper of the boat, Lt. Garcia had a leg injury, and a few of the crew were shaken up pretty bad. I called the other boat and warned them to stay back due to the reef. We would rig a line for them to pull us off in a few minutes.

They hooked up to our line and pulled us off, but we had a hole big enough in the bottom that you could crawl through. If the boat was moving it would not take on any water but when it slowed it started flooding in. The skippers agreed that they needed to get moving so they could save the boat with the hole and get the injured back for medical care.

I talked to the scouts and thought that with Baker injured we should abandon the sneak and peek, but they said that we were on a tight time schedule and had to go through with it. I decided to take Baker's place in the team since a few of his guys were down with injuries. It should be a cake-walk, right? I was in charge of the "Alpha Team," and First Lieutenant Jacobs was in charge of the "Bravo Team."

The teams got into the rubber boats and rowed themselves to shore, we did not take any PT-sailors this time since there was only a small garrison and we would deflate the boats and stash them in the undergrowth.

I carried the camera in a waterproof bag so it would not get ruined. We took soundings as we rowed into the beach. At the beach, we deflated the boats and covered them with palm leaves and marked it with a rock so we could find it the next night.

We walked around the island making notes when we came upon a machine gun nest manned by one man that was asleep at his post. One of the scouts slit his throat, and we moved the body off the trail and covered it up with a palm leaf, we made sure there was no evidence of us left to find.

If there was a sentry post this far out in the boonies, then there might be further ones up the trail, so we needed to watch out. We could see campfires up ahead, so we gave them a wide berth.

It was tough walking off the trail, but we needed to do it to complete the mission. We had to wade across a wide stream that looked like it was cutting the island in half. After about ½ of the team made it across one of our guys, Sgt. Brown got pulled under by a crocodile that was just under the surface, it had to be about twelve feet long and Sgt. Brown never had a chance. We tried to grab for him, and a few guys pulled them knives to try to attack the croc, but he was gone. The rest of the squad made it without incident.

After about three hours, we could see that it was getting light to the east so sun-up was around 05:00 so we needed to find a place with a good cover where we could see the enemy and not be seen by them. We found a small cave that was hidden from view by the foliage. We decided to take a break and eat some C-rats and drink some of our water.

The guys filed in and sat against the wall when 1st. Lt. Jacobs let out a stifled scream, he had been bitten by a small snake on the thigh, he just missed sitting on him. We turned our flashlights on and saw the snake go into a crevice in the rock. Jacobs was dead within a minute.

We dug a crude grave and buried him in the cave so Graves-Registration could find him later. I made a mark on the map to make it easier to find.

I did not know what was worse, fighting the japs or mother-nature. At least with the japs, they often yelled “BANZAI” when they attacked you, but mother-nature was tricky and silent.

We decided to make a clearing in the palm trees where we could keep an eye on anything that might want to bite us, sting us, or eat us. We would take four-hour shifts, sleeping and watching.

The scouts sent two men out to reconnoiter the area and draw some maps for me while the rest of us slept for a few hours.

When the second team came back, they had all kinds of surprises, including a sword! They had pictures of the base camp taken from the trees surrounding the base and drawings of the gun emplacements and locations that our Battleships and Cruisers could use to hit them with the big guns before the soldiers went ashore.

The planners were right when they said that this information would save lives of the troops coming ashore, if we could wipe out the gun emplacements in the pre-invasion bombing before any of our men hit the beaches, then they would not have to walk into a “shit-storm” of gunfire. They just needed to watch the wildlife.

We got all the information we needed and slept until it was getting dark again. We made our way back to the tree with the rock that marked where our boats were hidden. I helped dig the boats out of the leaves, and they got them re-inflated so they would float us back out when the PT boats arrived.

It was a little after midnight when we saw the red-light flash twice from a boat, we gave the three quick red response flashes and set out in the boats. We had all of our maps and drawings in water-proof bags, and I had three canisters of film to get developed when I got back to Australia.

We made it back to the PT-base, and I checked in with Baker at the medical tent, I was a little surprised to see Ramos was there waiting for me too. He said that Halsey was back and had heard what I had done to accomplish the mission and he was not too happy with me.

Ramos had arraigned for air transportation for us to get back to headquarters as quickly as we could, and the Admiral even sent fighter cover for our flight from his carrier in the area. I got the film over to the processing team as soon as we landed, and we went to see the Halsey in his office.

The Admiral asked me if I wanted to make it out of this war alive? I said, "Yes Sir, I did."

He asked me, what the hell did I think I was doing going behind enemy lines? He said pulling those kinds of stunts would shorten my life expectancy to a few weeks instead of years. He said that I could never go off in another PT boat because of the information that I know, if I was captured by the enemy, I would set the war effort back two years, besides did I not know that Full Captains did not go around leading Recon teams onto a jap held island!

I told him that I was sorry, I had only worried about getting the information and finishing the mission after Capt. Baker was injured and that I did not think about getting caught by the japs.

He told me to NEVER let it happen again. All I could say was, "Yes, sir!" and I left his office.

I asked Ivan if he noticed anything different about the Admiral today? He said, "Yes." His collar was heavier since he came back from Pearl Harbor. They had promoted him to a four-star Full Admiral during his visit with Nimitz.

Ivan had gone over to the photo section while I was in with Halsey and picked up the pictures after they were developed. Boy were they clear pics.

We were able to send a few copies off to the "Intelligence Section" to see if they could identify the jap commander that the scouts had swiped the sword from. They said that he was one of the Army ground commanders in-charge of the jap invasion force from the “Battle of Midway,” he had been transferred after the japs lost all of their carriers in the sea battle. He was sent to a small island garrison to redeem his family name.

We were not going to allow him to do that.

I took the pictures to Halsey, and he was amazed at how good they were. He called over to the General’s office to see if he could see him right away. He was going to take them over to MacArthur and see how soon the General could get his ground troops ready for a quick invasion.

Halsey knew that he had a fast attack carrier task force standing ready and they had two battleships that were two days steaming from the area.

The General said that he had a reinforced battalion that could load out on two-troop-ships tonight, and that their equipment and supplies were pre-loaded on LST-ships and they could be underway at daylight. Halsey said that his carriers were close enough that they could start bombing runs in the morning. It would take the troop ships one day to get to the island so the bombers could soften it up for twenty-four hours ahead of time, they would hold off on the battleships for another time.

It was amazing to see how fast things could move when it all came together, just the other day I was on an enemy-held island getting info for a future invasion, and today they were starting the wheels in motion to invade the island before the japs figured out what we were doing.

The Admiral and the General concurred that the time was ripe to jump early before the japs figured it out and sent more replacements to reinforce the garrison. If they were going to come, they would come from the Island of Truk, so he decided to send another carrier task force to that area to keep their heads down till our troops were dug in.

The next two days were really busy around the office. Ivan reminded me at breakfast that the troops were going ashore right now on my island, so we were all going to meet at the command center.

We had to wait until the incoming messages got decoded to find out that the bombers from the navy had all but wiped out the garrison on the island and even all the gun emplacements were wiped out.

The soldiers coming ashore were met with token resistance and secured the island in four hours. They even took fourteen prisoners, and one of them was the garrison commander that had lost his sword. He would never be able to redeem his family name now after becoming a prisoner of war.

Gen. MacArthur was really happy with how the planning and execution of the invasion came out, he said that we caught those damn japs with their tongues in the sake again. He also said that I was never to take another mission like the one I did with the scouts, he said that there was going to be a few medals for our part in the invasion.

One thing I was learning was that the Army was medal happy.

Chapter 13 - The Aircraft is on fire

I talked with Ivan over supper and told him that I needed him to take some plans for the next phase of our island hopping to the base commander at Bouganville and see if he has any questions. He said he would fly out in the morning.

I had other meetings so I could not go and besides the Admiral had warned me not to go anywhere up the slot because of what I knew about upcoming targets. So, the logical choice was Ivan, and we thought we had all the japs ran out of the Solomon Islands now.

Ivan took the plans we had and left the next morning for Guadalcanal first and then up the chain towards Bouganville. He stopped at another base on the way up the chain and dropped off a copy of the paperwork to Capt. Baker and his scouts, he told them he would come back and enjoy some homecooked C-Rats for dinner with them as soon as he finished on Bouganville. They had a good laugh about that joke.

By 19:00, Capt. Baker was getting worried because Ramos was supposed to be back by 16:00 so he sent off a message to Bouganville asking them if Ramos had dropped off his package this afternoon?

They sent back a message that they had not seen Cmdr. Ramos and that they had just assumed that he got delayed and would come the next day. Bakers hair on the back of his neck was tingling, something was not right. He let them know that the aircraft might be down, and they would send out a search party and head toward Rabaul. He asked them to send a search party his way and look for any indication of a "downed aircraft."

Capt. Baker sent a priority one message to my office letting me know that he thought Ramos' plane had gone down in "the slot" and that they were going to send out a couple of PT boats to start the search tonight and then add some aircraft when the sun came up.

The two PT-skippers that got the assignment were a couple that were at Melville when Ramos was there, so they knew him from school. Now, this was getting personal for them. They headed northwest up the slot looking for any lights from a lifeboat. If you hit the currents just right, you could float past any island and be swept right out to sea, never to be found or heard from again.

Baker was also able to get a "Black-Cat," a PBY Catalina that was based at Rabaul to fly down the slot. These planes could fly at 125 mph and run 2500 miles on a fill up so it could cover a lot of ocean, faster than a PT boat could.

#27- Courtesy of AWM-AU- by Wikipedia

These planes can land on the water since they are basically a flying boat with wings. It has some pontoons on the wing tips that fold down for a water landing and fold up for flying.

I told the Admiral what was up and he told me it was imperative that we either found Cmdr. Ramos dead or alive, I told him "alive" was my preference.

Ivan's plane was flying at 5000 feet when they had an engine fire on the port wing. The pilot feathered the engine and pulled the fire extinguisher handle to put out the blaze, it should have worked in about fifteen seconds, but it did not do the job. The fire spread to the wing, and the crew was told by the pilot to get ready to jump so that he could try to ditch the plane in the water.

They put on parachutes in record time and stood in the rear port side blister-window with a lifeboat in a package when the plane captain said to jump now! Ivan was the first one out the door with the package, and another officer was in the window when the plane exploded in a big ball of flame. The blast shoved the officer out the opening, but his parachute was on fire. He died when he hit the water. The crew in the plane were all killed by the explosion.

Ramos had pulled his chute, and the life raft package was tied to him by a strap, he watched the plane go down into the ocean, and the other officer hit the water with a sickening "thud." When Ramos hit the water, it was not that bad, but trying to get out from underneath the canopy and cut away the shroud lines was tougher than he realized. He swallowed a lot of water before he finished.

He found the life raft package self-inflated when it hit the water, now he had to figure out how to climb into it without swamping the boat. It took him half a dozen times to get into the one-man boat, and he had lost the folding oars during one of his attempts. Now to think about what he was going to do, he was adrift in the "slot" of the Solomon Islands and not really sure just where he was.

The plane had exploded on its way down, so his courier bag had gone to the bottom with it. It had extra weights in it to help it sink if the need arose. He was alive but alone, adrift at sea without any paddles. He started laughing because the only thing he could think of was the old saying "You are going up shit creek without a paddle."

He thought about his wife back home, how would Chelsea take the news of his passing. Who would be there to bring up his baby that she was going to have any time now? That thought made him mad, and he decided that he would not give up and leave her alone in the world to bring a baby up with only a picture of him to show the baby!

He decided to look for the stars to help guide him, he had been in these waters in a PT boat and had taken many "star-shots" to check their exact location. Now if he only had a map to plot his location, oh well, at least he could figure out his direction of travel.

He figured that he was moving around five knots toward the northwest and he could see some smudges on the horizon that were probably islands, but he did not know if they were friendly or jap-held. The last thing he wanted to do was to row up to one of the enemy islands that they had hopped over, and it would be held by a bunch of ticked off, hungry enemy soldiers that might cook him up for a white-meat stew for dinner.

He was floating towards one island, but he saw different signal fires burning and he knew that our Marines had better judgment than to show lights to the ocean, so he used his arms to try to paddle back into the prevailing current, at one time he even put his legs over the side while he laid on his stomach and kicked as hard as he could to propel himself along, then he remembered the sharks that swam around so freely, so he pulled his legs back in. He had to keep his spirits up, so he kept picturing his wife in her wedding dress waiting for him.

He made it back into the main current, so he decided to take a break and rest a little. He ate a chocolate bar and drank from a carton of water and then laid his head down, the waves were only running about one to two feet, so he was not worried about being tossed out while he slept.

He slept for about four hours, and he dreamt he was back on a plane, the engine sound, sounded so real, he opened his eyes and thought "Hey, I do hear an airplane." So, he got into the safety kit and tried to find something to use to flag them down. He found the flare gun but had a time figuring out just how to load it. They never taught this at the PT-School in Melville, R.I. When he got out of this, he would make damn sure this info was added to the class curriculum.

The plane was flying to the southeast and had flown out of range by the time he figured out how to operate the flare gun. He would be ready the next time one came by. There was a cloud cover now so he could not tell his location by the stars and clouds usually meant rain so he found a poncho-cover that would snap onto the raft to help keep him dry when it rained.

He got undercover just as it began to downpour and boy was it coming down in buckets. They used to love these kinds of rainstorms when they were on the islands, they would strip down and go into a clearing with a bar of soap and wash and rinse. You just had to hurry and rinse before the rain stopped, it would stop just as quick as it started here in the South Pacific. Those were the good old days of just running around sinking ships and killing japs.

He wondered if he should deep-six his uniform just in case he was picked up by the japs, he did not want them to know that he was a Navy Commander assigned to Admiral Halsey's headquarters staff. He could say that he lost his uniform when he was blown off his ship and that he was just a new officer assigned to the Deck Department. He knew how to chip and paint so the story might hold if he was rescued by the japs.

Our PT boats had been going up and down the different straits and channels, from island to island without seeing anything. The "Black-Cat" had made one trip and did not see anything and was turning around and flying back up the slot.

Ivan fell back asleep under the rain cover and did not notice that the rain had stopped and that he was drifting close to another island when he woke up his raft was nosed into a cove, and the sun was up. He thought well this could be a good thing. Ivan tied the rope holding the raft to a tree so that it would not float away.

He started walking down a trail hoping that he could find out what island he was on, he found trash left behind by some jap troops but nothing that would help him out. He was hot and tired, the temperature had to be close to 120 degrees, he wished now that he would have stayed by the water so he could cool off. He had been walking for about ninety-minutes when he heard japs talking in their sing-song language.

Now he ducked and hid under the roots of a large banyan tree that was just off the trail. He held his breath as four soldiers wearing loin-cloths and army hats and carrying one Ariska rifle with a bayonet that made the rifle look like it was six feet long, the other guys were carrying a fish net and an eight-foot pole with a catch net on the end. They were walking back down the trail he had just come up, boy I hope they are not going to my cove he thought so he followed them.

They were heading for his cove for sure, right where his raft was tied up, he was really "up shit creek without a paddle" now and without a rifle too. They waded into the water and started fishing, they laid the net out on the bottom of the beach and waded out until they ran out of line. The soldier with the rifle laid it against a tree and climbed into the water with his friends to help them pull the net back in with the fish trapped as the water ran out.

They started pulling in the net to catch breakfast or lunch, or whatever, they had a full net when they turned around and saw the one-man raft tied under the tree.

The soldier that had left the rifle tried to swim/run toward the rifle, but Ivan beat him to the punch. He grabbed the rifle and chambered a round. He pointed it at the four men and indicated that they were his prisoners and they should put their hands up in the air.

They smiled and started jibber-jabbering in that sing-song language, and Ramos told them to, "Shut the hell up!" They shut up, so he asked them if they spoke any English. One of them spoke a little English, so Ivan told them to climb out of the water slowly and tie each other up to the tree.

The guy that spoke English said that they wanted to surrender to the Americans so that they could get some food and medical treatment like the papers from "heaven" told them they would. Ivan remembered that they were dropping leaflets on the islands that were hopped over saying that if they gave themselves up, they would receive food and medicine and be taken back home again.

We did not tell them they would not go home until the war was over, that was in the "fine print" and if they could not read it because they all wore "coke- bottle" glasses that was their problem, not Ivan's. Now he had to figure out what he was going to do on an enemy-held island with his four prisoners.

He made sure they were tied up so they could not get away, the last thing he wanted was for them to get to their buddies and have him for dinner.

He let the fish go so he could use the net to help tie up the four soldiers better. He wished he would have floated up to a friendly island, he could have been on his way back to Australia by now.

Ivan felt sorry for the soldiers so he tied them up to the base of the tree so they could lay down and sleep while he thought of his options. He had a few extra chocolate bars so he would share them with them when they woke up.

Later that night he thought he heard the Packard engines of a PT boat and then he heard it again, it was cruising up his strait and coming past his spot. He got into the Safety-Pak and pulled out a red-lensed, handheld flashlight, and he flashed it out to sea toward the sound of the boat. The engines took on a different tone, they slowed down and put on the mufflers and then came to a stop.

A red light flashed from the boat, in Morse-Code, they sent the word, "IDENTIFY." So, Ivan did the best he could, he barely passed the semaphore classes at Melville, but he did pass. He sent back by flasher light, "Ramos, USN, Airplane crashed." They told him to row out to them so he tied the prisoners to the raft and told them they were going to get the food and medical treatment they wanted, but they had to help swim and push the boat out to the edge of the coral shoal so they could get picked up.

They kicked for all of their lives, they wanted to be also saved, and Ivan steered the one-man boat the best he could. It took them almost one hour to swim out and then they were all pulled unto the PT boat. The skipper welcomed Ivan aboard and had the prisoners tied up to the radio mast with an armed guard to watch over them.

Ivan would be back to base in three hours, and they would arrange for a flight back in the morning after he was checked out by the "Doc" at the base.

On the trip back to the base, Ivan found out just how much Admiral Halsey cared for him, how many people did you know that had a "dead or alive" wanted poster put out with his own picture on it.

They handed the prisoners over to a marine guard when they got to the base, and the japs even thanked Ivan for saving their lives and taking them off their island. Ramos was checked out by the Doc and given a clean bill of health and told that there was a PBY-Catalina on the way to pick him up, it would be here in eight hours and take him straight to Australia with a Corsair Fighter Patrol to fly cover for him for the first leg and then the Army Air Corps took over with their P-38 Lightning (the fork-tailed devils as the japs called them).

The guys assigned to the base did not know who this officer was, but they could tell from the size of the search party that was trying to find this guy, that he was important to someone way up the chain-of-command and it was obviously over their pay-grade so, they did not ask any questions. The old saying "Yours is not to question why yours is to do or die" was the saying today.

They assigned a marine guard to stay with Ivan until his flight out. He asked for a bed to lay down for a little bit, so they put him up in the visiting officer's hut. He did not know what all the fuss was about, but it was fun to go with the tide.

The Marine guard woke him up at 06:00 and told him they had breakfast ready as soon as he was cleaned up and that his plane was due to land in about thirty to forty-five minutes.

It was almost eight hours flying time, so Ivan spent his time sleeping with a parachute on and buckled up, he told the crew that he wanted to be ready the next time. The crew woke him up twice and served him a box meal they had brought along for him, he was a little shaky during the flight, but the crew knew that his last flight ended in a crash, so they did not mention anything about it. They were friends with the plane crew that had died in the explosion and crash, and they knew that it could be them on any flight, so they were counting their blessings today and mourning the loss of some good friends again.

Chapter 14 - Returned to Halsey

Ivan landed just a little after 15:00 and the Admiral had him sent first to the medical officer for clearance, and then the Army debriefing team to tell them what had happened and what he could remember.

He showed up at our office around 18:00, he was looking pretty chipper until I told him the Admiral wanted to see him before he left for the night. He looked like a kid caught with his hand in the proverbial "cookie jar." I told him not to worry, the Admiral knew it was not his fault that his plane caught fire.

He spent about thirty minutes with Halsey and then joined me in the ante-room that went out to the balcony next door to the Admiral's office.

I told him we could go to the officer's club, they had fish tonight! He laughed and said that he would rather have a PB & J sandwich.

The next morning, we were back at it, we needed to make more copies of the original plans that went into the ocean with Ivan and get a different courier to take the plans up the slot. Ivan said that he was a little gun-shy about flying now.

I found an army Major that was willing to take the plans up to the base commanders that still needed them, he flew out that afternoon. I threw out an idea to the Admiral that maybe he needed to move his office up the slot to be closer to the action but still be a safe distance away from the fighting, he said that he and "The General" were just talking about that same idea.

They had requested that an old tender be converted to a command ship with plenty of office spaces and multi-radio rooms to be able to handle the message traffic that SO-WEST-PAC would need. They would have the photography guys on-board and even printing presses to make the copies we needed.

I reminded the Admiral to have a large enough galley on board to be able to feed everyone if we were under-way. He told me that he had found a cook that had been on the island of Rabaul cooking for the base commander that even knew how to make Baked Alaskan. I smiled at Ramos, and we both said at the same time "could it be" and laughed. No more Peanut Butter sandwiches were all I could think of. Ivan told me later that day that he was thinking of asking for a transfer, but with our cook coming back to us it might be worth it to stick around a little more.

We were in old buildings in New Caledonia that Admiral Halsey had moved into when he was sent down by Nimitz to take over from Admiral Ghormley on 18 October 1942 after Ghormley failed to lead the troops he had under him and Nimitz fired him.

Ghormley was on a small command ship and had never left the pier-side, and he was afraid of the French Governor on the island who would not allow him any office space in town. When Admiral Halsey took over, he went into town and evicted the VICHY-FRENCH from their embassy and took it over. He had plenty of room to operate from now.

One of the first things Admiral Halsey did when he took over was to call in all the commanders he had and asked them what they needed to hold their positions? He took their answers and promised them everything he had coming would get to them, and he kept his promises. That is one reason that the troops really liked having "Bull" Halsey in command of the SW-PAC area. He respected them, and they respected him back and proved it by doing whatever he needed to be done.

We moved into the command ship in December and made plans to move away from New Caledonia and go up the slot towards Rendova, this would get us closer to the action so we could stay on top of situations as they developed. We could check in with different commands as we needed to and not endanger anyone to fly up the slot or take a PT boat to different islands. This might get interesting again.

The Army had started using P-38 Lightning as photo-recon planes to take pictures of the island defenses that we would be going up against, this stopped Capt. Baker and his band of scouts from going in on an enemy-held island to map out the gun positions.

With the speed of the airplanes, they could develop the film and have bombers on the way within two to three hours after the overflight landed. The planes flew high enough that the enemy would not even know that they were being photographed and the pictures were crystal clear. The photo-teams could interpret the images and show the bomber crews just what they were targeting. They would catch the enemy before they could have time to move any gun placements to a new location.

It sped up our timeline from three to six months to gather info and pictures and plan an upcoming invasion down to one month now. We were finally moving faster than the enemy could move in response to our attacks. And with our command and control ship being with-in 100 miles of the action we could get the info we needed to the front lines as quick as possible.

When they refurbed the ship, I made sure they would have plenty of anti-aircraft guns installed and a crew to man them. We pulled daily drills until the men could load the guns in their sleep, I felt sorry for any jap that came within range of those guns.

We were making good tracks up the back of the Guinea Bird and the next island we would take after Biak was called Morotai. The pictures from the P-38s was a big help in all the planning sessions we had.

The Admiral called me into his office one day and told me that he was going to be relieved as the commander of the SO-WEST-PACIFIC area and sent to command the Third Fleet Task Force in the Pacific Ocean. Within six months, we would be back into the Philippines so that General MacArthur could finish his pledge to the Filipino Nationals that "He Would Return."

Halsey said that Admiral Nimitz wanted him to be at the front of the Naval war that was brewing in the Central Pacific now that the majority of the SW-Pacific was finished.

He told me that I could ask for any new assignment when we were finished, and he would get it granted, and the same went for Ivan Ramos, he said that he could have never done all that we accomplished in the last year without us working as a team.

Ivan almost fell out of his chair when I told him about my meeting with Halsey, and he said that he was thinking about going back to Melville to be an instructor again, I told him I was thinking the same thing. We both laughed at that one.

He wondered if Halsey was going to take the cook with him or if we could steal him away? I told him he was probably going to go with the Admiral as his personal cook, what a way to go through a war.

It was Sunday afternoon, and the Admiral was on the beach that afternoon talking to the men when the radio speakers blared out "CONDITION RED," and the air-raid sirens started wailing on the island. The ship went to General Quarters, and the gun crews manned the anti-aircraft stations.

The PT boats that were with us got underway so as to be a smaller target for the japs that were coming at us. How I wish I was with them instead of being cooped up on this ship. I told Ivan I was going up on deck to help direct the anti-aircraft fire and that he needed to send out a message that we were under fire and ask for fighter support from a local airfield.

There were four PT boats that got underway, and they were already firing at the 10 or so jap fighters that were escorting about a dozen bombers. I got in a gun-tub with a BO-FORS 40mm and assisted the gun crew by directing them to the closest airplanes.

#28 US Navy Photo Courtesy of Wikipedia

They were a fine-tuned crew, and I might have been more in the way, so I decided to help with hauling the ammo up to them. The ships' crew got four of the fighters when they came close enough, and the PT boats were able to direct enough fire-power at the bombers that all the bombs were dropped short of the targets. One of the fighters was on fire and was shooting at us as he went over, four guys from the gun crew were injured including me and three were killed.

I took a 5.7 cal. machine gun round in my right leg just as I was jumping behind a shield with another shipmate, he was a step behind me and took three rounds in the back. He died in my arms, I bet he was only seventeen years old. He was so young, yet he never cried, he just told me to "get that sum-bitch" for him. I told him we got him, as he took his last breath.

There were other crewmen that came along and carried us to the First-Aid station where the corpsman was waiting to bandage us up. They had enough wounded that they decided to take us ashore to the doctors at the new base hospital.

They were able to stop the bleeding right away on the ship or else I would have bled to death before the doctor got to me, the bullet went through the femoral artery, so they put a tourniquet on me. The round that hit me must have ricocheted off of a steel panel because it tumbled in at an odd angle and broke the femur bone as it went through the leg. The doctor said that if it would have hit me full force that it might have taken the leg right off.

I was laying on an operating table when I woke up before the surgery and saw this corpsman putting things on a tray, and I said "Hey there, can I get a blanket? I am kind of cold here." He took one look at me and yelled out. The anesthesiologist came running in and put a mask on my face and said, "Nighty-night." I woke up two days later after the surgery.

It took me a while to get the fog cleared out of my head, but then I saw Ivan sitting there in a chair, and I told him we needed to postpone the Monday morning meeting before everyone got there and we were not ready. He laughed and said, "Good Morning Sunshine," and that today was Tuesday, and that we already had the Monday morning meeting.

He said that Halsey wanted to know as soon as I was awake so he could stop by to see me. I told him to let me get decent first, so he left and sent in a corpsman to help me get cleaned up and shaved. My right leg was in a full cast so I could not put on a pair of pants so we did the best we could do with a clean robe. They changed the sheets and made the bed and put me in a chair before the Admiral came in. They brought in another couple of chairs for any other visitors.

The Admiral came in about an hour later with his chief of staff and a couple of junior officers. I tried to stand out of duty, but he laughed and said, "As you were Captain." I tried to set at attention as best I could.

Halsey told me he had a lot of respect for any officer that would put himself in danger and help direct the gun-crew and even help them carry ammo so they would not run dry during an air-attack. He said that he had the whole story from the crew that was around me and that he was saddened about those guys that did not make it.

I told him that I could not in good conscious just stand around while those jap bastards were gunning at my shipmates. He said that by sending Ivan off to the radio shack allowed the aircrews on the next island north of us to intercept the air-raid and they were able to shoot down every one of the planes.

With the four planes that our gunners were able to get on our ship and the four planes that the PT boats got, that left fourteen planes that our fighters were able to down in the drink without a loss to our aircrews.

Halsey told me that he was putting me in for a medal for Bravery and that I would be getting the Purple Heart for the leg injury. I said, "Thank you, sir."

He said that he was going to arrange for Ivan and I both to be sent to Melville, R.I. as instructors at the PT-School after our thirty-day leave. He said that when I have recuperated enough to travel, I will be sent to Australia first to get another couple of medals from "Dug-out-Doug" and then off to Pearl Harbor to see Nimitz before my free trip home.

I did not know if the medicines were making my head spin or all the news that Halsey was giving me, so he told me to go back to sleep and that was an order.

The next day Ivan came by to see me and told me that there was already a new replacement officer for both of us, so he was spending his time making sure they were both on the same page with Halsey and his wishes.

Halsey said that he did not yet know who his replacement commander would be since the SW-PACIFIC area was shrinking smaller and smaller every week as we took new islands and bypassed others to wither away on the vine.

I told Ivan that I would be ready to travel in about a week so he said that would work for him because he had shown the new guys everything he could and that Halsey did not like them anyway, so it was great timing for us to leave now. He said that he brought me a snack from the chef, and he produced a peanut butter and jelly sandwich out of his bag, we had a good laugh.

They wanted me to stay in a wheelchair as much as possible, but I told them flying, and a wheelchair was not going to be possible, so Ivan procured a set of crutches and Halsey provided his plane for us to make our trip, first to see the General and then to Pearl Harbor.

The General pinned three different medals on Ivan and me and said that a Letter of Commendation was being put in our service jackets, he said those letters and 10 cents would get a cup of coffee for us stateside!

We flew out of there on Friday and made Pearl Harbor around noon on Saturday, we had a tail-wind that helped us along at a good clip all the way into Hawaii.

I had mixed emotions about leaving the war behind, but in our meeting with Nimitz, he set my feelings at ease, by first telling us that we had done so much to help with the allied effort in the SW-Pacific area that he was really proud of us. He said not to think that we were leaving the war and our shipmates behind but to consider that we were going home to train the next new classes of PT-officers to take the war to the enemies' doorstep.

He said that "Bull Halsey" was good at seeing potential in a person and that we set the bar high for the others that would follow in our footsteps. The next phase of the war was not going to need as many PT boats until we got to the Philippine Islands themselves, maybe a year from now. He said that then, they were going to be a force to reckon with and the japs would be sorry they ever started this war.

We said our good-byes and a driver took us to the officer's club for supper and then to the airport to catch our flight to San Diego. It was a bumpy flight this time due to weather that was blowing in from the ocean, but we got in at 09:00. We ate some breakfast after checking in for our next flight.

My leg was starting to hurt so Ivan made some arraignments for me to lay down for a little bit and elevate my leg. It helped to be in our dress uniforms with all the medals on your chest, and I was on crutches too.

We had front of the line privileges on this trip due to strings that Nimitz had pulled on our travel orders. I even got two seats so that I could stretch my leg out during the flight to Chicago, boy did I get some nasty stares from the other servicemen on the plane, but when they saw all the “salad” on my chest and my four gold Captain stripes on my jacket, they backed off. It did not hurt any that Ivan is the size of a football full-back and he was my bodyguard.

Nimitz had arraigned for a Navy “puddle-jumper” to take us to South Bend Field since it was going to pick up some critical parts from the Studebaker Truck Plant in South Bend and return to Chicago Field. I had wired my dad to have a car with a big back seat since I had a broken leg and was in a cast. I would explain it to him on the trip home.

Dad showed up first so I told Ivan that I would meet him in Melville in twenty-eight days. On the trip home, dad was quiet, he was waiting on me to open the conversation, I told him about what had happened and how I had gotten hurt. I reassured him that I was ok and that the leg was healing ok also. He said that he was just worried about my head, was it still screwed on straight or not?

I told him I was ok in that department. Also, we still had a war to fight only now I was going to fight it from the PT-school in Melville, R.I.

Mom put on one of her famous pot-roast dinners for all the family and friends. They must have pooled all their food ration coupons together to make it work, but it was better than I could remember. Dad even did home-made vanilla ice cream on top of mom's homemade blueberry pie. I told them that I had not had any ice cream since the time that Admiral Halsey had sent it to us after we had saved the pilots that ditched at sea.

Then they all wanted to hear the story of that saga. I had to cut out any locations that they might have heard on the newsreels at the movie house on Saturday afternoon, after all, we were still at war.

We had a good time laughing at some of the things I had gone through in this war. They loved the stories I shared about running the boats up and down the slot and then working with Admiral Halsey in Australia and the Slot. My mom could not get over that "Bull" Halsey knew her little boy, she said she could not wait till the next week's bible study at church so she could top her friend Ruby's stories of her son in Europe!

I had to remind her that we were still at war, so she needed to be careful what all she shared with her women's group at the bible study, after-all just how well did she know this "Ruby", maybe her real name was "Rubinski," and she was from Russia not really South Bend. Mom slapped me on the arm and said do not tease like that, young man! It made us all have a good laugh

Chapter 15 - A New Admiral in the works

I had the option of going up to Great Lakes Recruit Training Center, north of Chicago, to get my cast off, or I could just see my local family doctor, it would take 1-month of fuel ration coupons to make the trip since I did not have a navy car at my disposal so to save time and coupons I decided just to use my family doctor.

These coupons were difficult to come up with and if you went through a tire or broke something else you were not going to be driving anywhere since the rubber was being used to make tires for the military and the car plants were not turning out spare parts for civilians. My doctor had taken good care of me all my life so far, so I figured that he could take an x-ray and cut off the cast for me when it was time.

I waited until the day before I was to leave for Melville to get the cast off so it would give it extra time to heal. The x-ray came back good, so the doctor had the cast cut off, now I needed to start exercising to rebuild the muscle that shrunk due to non-use during the last two months. I was sure that the gym at Melville would be fine for that.

The doctor told me to use a cane until I could walk without it, he thought four weeks would be about right and to work out daily to exercise it.

I caught a flight out of South Bend Field to Detroit Naval Air Station and then into New York. I found a Navy bus to Philadelphia Navy Yard and then changed over to a bus that was going to

Melville with a group of new PT-sailors. These guys were really surprised when a Four-Striper got onboard with them for the ride to Melville. It took us right up to the Administration Building after checking in with the sentry at the front gate.

I could not believe how much the school had grown since I had been there as a student. I was being assigned to a senior officer billet and would share a small hut with five other guys including Ivan.

Ramos was due in on the next morning's bus, so I beat him here this time. I would have to razz him about him being my assistant, but that I got there first, and set up our room! He had better shape up, or I might have to put him on thirty days peanut butter and jelly!

I found out that we would be worked into the regular teaching curriculum with the next class that would start in two weeks so until then we could sit in with any class, we wanted to so we could see how they taught them today versus when we went through the class in 1942.

I was going to be teaching the Senior Officers at first, and Ivan was going to be teaching the new Executive Officers, we both would be teaching single boat and group tactics to them. These were limited classes that only went for thirty days, and then these officers would be going back out to the war.

One night some of the other instructors wanted to know who I was related to, in order to get these cushy assignments, I said who, you mean uncle Franklin? Then I smiled and told them that I was a nobody before I came into the boats, but then all I did was my duty, and that was all that was expected of them from here on out.

After that, they started treating me as if I was one of the groups again. My leg had gotten stronger because Ivan made me go work out and run with him at the end of the day. I reminded him that I had never worked out that much even as a PT-Skipper and he said that was probably why I was only on a 50% scholarship to Notre Dame, and he was on a 100% full ride for football.

I told him that I would race him tonight to see who buys supper, he said you are on. So, at 18:00 we put on our tennis shoes and shorts and took off on a two-mile run around the base. Ivan beat me by about twenty feet to the finish line at the main gate. I told him he cheated, but he laughed all the way to the barracks. I could not believe how fast he was for how big he was, that guy had some serious leg muscles on him.

We added a couple of items in our classes for the students, first was how to survive in the jungle, the second was how to evade the enemy, and the third was how to resist if you were captured and fourth was how to use a flare gun. I told the students that it was always a good idea to have a small survival pouch on your gun-belt with a little water-proof compass included in it, it would come in handy if they lost their boat and they got to an island.

I told them about the current bounty on a skipper's head if you were captured, just that information popped some of their bubbles about becoming a war hero. I related Ivan's story about his airplane crash and making it to an enemy-held island. This is where the survival gear would come in handy.

We arraigned for everyone to take a turn in the bay getting into a 1-man raft and paddling it to shore. The base commander said that taking a parachute class was not needed since most of them would never even see an airplane during their time in the service.

We were able to tie all of our experiences together with the class curriculum and had it make more sense to them, instead of just learning how to drive and operate a PT boat.

All the new boats were coming equipped with a 37 mm anti-barge gun and with radar, I told the class of how we lashed our "borrowed" anti-tank gun to a couple of two-by-six boards on the bow in order to sink the jap barges. And these new radar units would come in handy in finding the enemy when they were trying to hide around an island.

I did not know all the new information on the use of radar, so I listened just like the students when the radar technicians taught the class for us.

We even went out into the bay at night on the boats from squadron #4 that were assigned to the school and practiced with the radar units on ships coming and going. I set up a practice run on a couple of navy landing boats that were about the size of an enemy barge.

It was amazing how detailed the scope was when it came to the barge, we had the navy coxswain float the landing boat up next to the shoreline so we could see how it differed from the land mass. That would have been nice to have when we were in the Solomon Islands.

Ivan and I had spent almost a year at the school, and we knew that the war was winding down, General MacArthur was getting ready to go back to the Philippines again, so we were moving most of our PT boats to that area. We had retaken all the South-West Pacific islands that the Japanese had taken in the first year of the war. In the Central-Pacific area, Admiral Halsey was kicking butt also with his Carrier Task Forces.

I had gotten a message this morning from Admiral Halsey and was going to open it at lunch with Ivan. It was stamped Top-Secret, For My Eyes Only, that is why I waited to open it in private with Ramos.

Halsey's message said that he wanted to invite both of us back to the war! The Navy was going to ramp up the use of PT boat squadrons around the thousands of islands that made up the Philippines, and he wanted someone with our qualifications to help lead the march into Tokyo Bay with him.

He was asking us to put in for a transfer to Ulithi Atoll in the Carolinas Island group. U.S. Forces landed in Sep. 1944 and began building one of the largest naval bases used in the war. At its peak, Ulithi Atoll housed 617 ships, had its own 1200-yard airstrip, and hosted 20,000 troops on its recreation island, Mogmog.

#29 US Navy Photo- Public Domain by Wikipedia

They had ten floating dry-docks that could handle ships up to a battleship or a carrier to fix any underwater repairs needed.

#30 US Navy Photo- Public Domain -- Provided by Wikipedia

They had a million-gallon fueling station that provided fuel barges that went from ship to ship so that they did not have to shift anchorages just to top off with fuel-oil. The fuel tankers would even go along with the task-force to re-fuel at-sea. The US Navy had perfected this tactic, but the japs had not.

The Navy was growing with new ships being delivered every month, so they needed the support facilities to take care of them, and our Seabees were up to the tasks.

I asked Ivan what he thought of going back to the war zone? He just smiled that goofy smile. I said ok, I would put in a request and send off a reply to Admiral Halsey that he had his two boys back.

Halsey sent a message back to me saying that we would meet up at Ulithi the next time he got in and that I would report to Admiral Jackson who was in charge of the Island. He would make all the connections we needed to be there by the first of next month, this would give us time to see the families again on our trip out. He said that at least part of the trip to Ulithi would be by aircraft carrier out of Hawaii, but that we would be living in the flag quarters while on-board so we would not be interacting with the rest of the crew. He also said that he was asking Nimitz to promote Ramos to Captain and me to Admiral (lower half). I fell out of my chair at that sentence.

I knew that all promotions to Admiral had to have the ok from Congress and the President of the United States, so we will see what happens when we get to Hawaii.

We both said good-bye to Melville and went home for a quick stop over, I did not tell the folks about the future promotion because I did not know if it would get approved yet.

We landed at Pearl Harbor and was ushered to a driver that took us right to see Admiral Nimitz. He told us that the promotion had been approved by the President and he gave me his first pair of gold stars and said that they brought him good luck and maybe they would do the same for me. I thanked him and had Ramos put them on my shirt and then I put my Captains eagle on Ivan for him. Nimitz said that we would be leaving in two days for Ulithi and that he was going with us, so that was why we would be living in the Flag Quarters on the carrier.

Nimitz said that he wanted to set up an advance office when we got to Guam so he wanted to visit Ulithi Atoll and then he would fly back to Guam and spend the rest of the time running the war from there. He said that the Seabees would have his new office and quarters finished by the time we got there.

He was looking forward to being away from all the reporters that kept wanting to speak to him at Pearl, he was a quiet person and liked to think more than he liked to speak so the peace and quiet would do him good. The Navy could control the civilian population on Guam a lot better than they could on Hawaii.

I told Ivan that we needed to go to the base uniform center to get new stripes sewed on our jackets, he could have all my shoulder boards with the four solid stripes but that I needed to get the one solid strip for an Admiral added to my uniforms.

He said that I could afford the gold with my pay-raise! I told him that I would spring for lunch at the officer's club after we went to the uniform center.

We had a nice lunch and got really good tables that are usually reserved for senior officers on an outside veranda looking out over the submarine base. We could even order more than one drink with our meals now.

I told Ivan that I wanted to check onboard the new carrier in the morning even though we still had another day before they pulled out. This would allow us time to find our way around before Nimitz got on-board. He agreed with me.

We got to the carrier at 09:00, and they even rang me aboard as "Motor- Torpedo-Boat-Division-2 Commander- Arriving," now that surprised me because Nimitz did not say anything about a title going with the stripe. We were given a marine escort to our quarters, and they said that someone would be available at all times to take us anywhere we needed to go on the ship. Or we could just ask the steward for anything, and they would get it for us.

We even had a Flag Cook assigned to cook for us all. There were going to be four other Admirals on board with us for this trip, Nimitz and Spruance and their staffs would be traveling with us. Spruance was on his way out to relieve "Bull Halsey" for six months.

The US Navy started changing out the Admiral of the task force instead of all the ships in the task forces, they would only change the command number, like Halsey was Commander 7th fleet and Spruance was Commander 9th fleet. This also kept the japs wondering how many fleets we had available.

At the start of the war we only had two to three carriers available for the whole Pacific war zone, now we were up to twenty fast fleet carriers (CV's) and around forty-five escort carriers (CVE). The escorts were used to fly replacement aircraft over to the fleet carrier, and they were not armored against enemy shelling or aerial bombing, they had wood flight decks to save weight. The CVE's carried a nick-name of "Combustible, Very Expendable" That is why they tended to stay back away from the front lines

We shifted ships colors at 16:00 and got underway for Ulithi. Nimitz and his staff got onboard about thirty minutes before we left and our marine escort said that the Admiral wanted to see us at 17:00, on his Flag Bridge. I had to ask him what was the uniform of the day to see the Admiral.

The Sgt. said that if we wore our Kaki work uniforms, we would fit in nicely with all the other brass. I told him I was new at having a star on my collar he said "No! I would have never guessed that sir" and we both chuckled at that.

He was going to be able to teach me a lot during this trip. I told him that like a Navy Chief actually runs the navy, a Sargent was the one that ran the Marines. He said, "I knew I would like you, the first time I saw you, sir!"

Sgt. Becker led us up to the Flag bridge and stood aside so that we could pass through the hatch before him, Admiral Nimitz was talking to Admiral Spruance over a planning table that had a map on it, so he stopped and introduced us to everyone around the room.

He told us that the information we were about to be let in with was ULTRA-TOP-SECRET and was not to be shared with anyone other than those in this room. What he was showing us was the preliminary plans for the invasion of the Philippine Islands

MacArthur wanted to return in January 1945, but he was worried that the japs had a large airbase on Palau's island group, with the largest two islands being Peleliu and Angaur, he wanted a US Airbase on Peleliu to protect his right flank, so we were planning that attack to start in mid-September. The Seabees would start on enlarging the airfield as soon as the island was secured.

Nimitz and MacArthur did not get along when it came to tactics needed to end the war. Nimitz wanted to jump past the Philippines and attack Formosa, but MacArthur wanted to go back to the Philippines to save face and promote his up-coming political career, he was already threatening President Roosevelt with running against him in the upcoming election.

MacArthur won the President over, and Nimitz had to take the back seat. They were moving most of the 7th fleet back under Nimitz's control since they were not needed in the south-west Pacific, but they would play a large part in the invasion of the Philippines starting in September.

Nimitz said that I would have a command ship at my disposal to run the PT boats around the Philippine islands, I would go on-board at Ulithi and follow the fleet westward. He said that we already had twenty-four boats ready to start operations around the south of Mindanao and that more were on the way. They would start harassing the japs coming through the Celebs Sea into the Sulu Sea, the japs felt more protected by staying in the South China Sea west of the islands instead of the Philippine Sea on the east side of the Philippines.

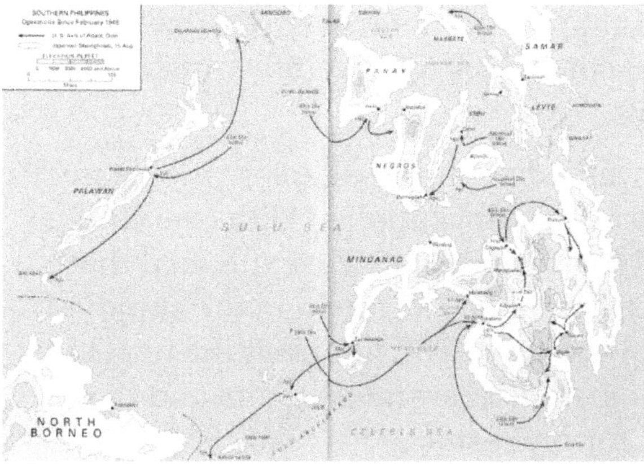

#31 map provided by Wikipedia

They did not know that we were sending a dozen submarines into that area in the next week. One of the main jap navy bases for refueling the capital ships was in Borneo, at the oil terminals at Balikpapan that the Dutch did not blow up when they fled ahead of the jap invasion. Some of the oil fields were blown up, but the Army got caught by the japs that landed ten miles up the coast and came in by road instead of from the ocean as they thought they would. A large oil terminal was left alone by the army when they fled for their lives.

The fuel oil from Borneo was so pure coming right out of the ground that they did not even have to refine it before they put it in the ships. This fuel was like pure gold to any navy that got ahold of it to fuel their ships. If we could take Borneo away from the japs, we would save a lot of time from shipping our fuel tankers from Australia or even from Hawaii or the US.

We had another couple of planning sessions with Nimitz in his at-sea cabin, he said that Halsey was going to Pearl for about five months to rest while Admiral Spruance took over the chase. The “Bull” would come back to hopefully finish the war in Tokyo Bay.

Nimitz wanted me to get aggressive with my PT boats and to keep them supplied with everything they needed to finish the job. He explained that Ramos was going to be a big help in the supply department because he did not want me to get tied down with logistics, he wanted results and that I was known, for my results.

I asked him if we were running two boats as a team or as a flotilla? He said that both would be acceptable, I would have to look at the area we are trying to cover but to use stealth instead of just roaming around looking for the enemy.

He told me that the information he was about to share with me had to go with me to the grave if need be, I told him that I understood. He opened a file that was marked “ULTRA” and showed me radio traffic that had been intercepted and decoded from the japs.

He said that we could read the jap code faster than they could decode it and that it would be quicker for the japs to ask us what was sent to them. My mouth was open, and he laughed and said that I was catching flies.

Now some of our previous attacks in the Solomon Islands were making sense, how else would we know that a certain number of jap ships were coming down the slot at a certain time and date and that they were on time. I asked him if that was how we won at Midway Island, he smiled and said that was the tipping point for us.

We were able to read the battle order from Admiral Yamamoto to his ships, and everything told us where they would be and when they would be there, and the rest is now history. He said that I would be read into any message traffic that involved my area of responsibility and that I could tell my PT-Commanders what to do but that I could not say anything about where I got the information from. If you have to you will tell them that a coast-watcher passed on the information to us. I answered with an "Aye, Aye, Sir."

He wanted to know if I could pull it off?

I said, "Can-Do Sir."

He smiled and told me to take a break, we would be in Ulithi in about twelve hours, and then the fun would start all over again. He said that Halsey was in port onboard the Enterprise and that we would meet for breakfast at 07:00, in his quarters. He said that he had asked his wife to send an extra jar of strawberry preserves for me since I liked it so much the last time we met, and he knew that Halsey would have home-made biscuits with the eggs, so we would take the Admirals gig at 06:30 over to the "Big E" to have our pow-wow with Halsey.

Sgt Becker took me back to my stateroom and asked if there was anything else that I needed? I told him that I could use a haircut and needed to have my uniforms cleaned before my meeting with Halsey in the morning. He told me to change into a clean work khaki uniform and that he would send the barber up to my stateroom and return my clothes, cleaned and pressed so that even a marine would be impressed with my creases.

I packed my bags and got ready to have breakfast with our "favorite" Admiral in the morning on his flag-ship. I made sure that Ivan was ready to go also.

Chapter 16 - My own Command Ship

Our ship had pulled in and anchored only about 2000 yards away from the Enterprise, so it only took us about fifteen minutes to go over, Nimitz had told Sgt. Becker to have my bags and Ivan's' sent over to the Mount McKinley Command ship and that we would be along in about three hours.

Admiral Halsey was his normal self, you could tell that the war was wearing on him, he had lost weight since the last time we worked together, and he had more salt than pepper in his hair. He commented that the chow at Melville must have agreed with me because I looked like I needed some time in the base gym.

I told him that was on the agenda as soon as I got set up on-board the Mount McKinley, he smiled and said the biscuits were fresh out of the oven so we could eat anytime Nimitz was ready. Nimitz pulled out the Preserves from his pouch that his chief of staff set down next to him and said that he was ready if the coffee was hot.

We went over the initial plans for me to set up my command and that my staff was already on-board my ship, I would meet them this morning after breakfast.

The Admiral allowed me to use his gig to get over to my new ship, they had replaced his five-star flag with a one star for me. When I took my first step onto the accommodation ladder from the gig, they rang the ships bell with five gongs and said over the ships and MC announcing system "Motor-

Torpedo-Boat Division two, Arriving," and then one gong when I stepped onboard the quarter-deck. I saluted the Officer of the Deck and asked for permission to come aboard.

The Captain of the ship was there to greet me along with "side-boys" to make it official.

I had six officers for my staff, from Commander on down to Lieutenant and even an Ensign, they had all worked on PT boats in the past. Maybe this would be a cake-walk as Capt. Baker used to say.

Ramos told me that the latest message traffic he had seen was that we would pull out at 21:00 after they had finished fueling us. There was going to be another twelve ships going with us to our new base north on the island of Halmahera which was situated between the head of New Guinea and the closest Philippine Island of Davao on the southern tip.

Our first attacks would be directed at any jap shipping that was trying to go through the Celebes Sea to the Sulu Sea, on the north-eastern tip of Borneo. There were hundreds of mini-islands in and around the Palawan Passage, and we were going to set up some ambushes for the japs.

I wanted to let the Submarine Headquarters in Australia know that we were open for business and that we were both on the same team, so they needed to let their subs know to watch out for our PT boats and I would let the boat commanders know to make "damn sure" that it was NOT a US Navy submarine before they fired any torpedoes at a sub on the surface.

I instructed my people that a General Court Marshal proceeding would be ordered for "Negligence" against any skipper that killed a US Sub while under my command. They would not only have to live with the deaths of fellow US Navy Sailors on their conscious, but they would live with it, in Leavenworth Prison.

Ramos thought that was a good one, just like me telling my crews that they would be shot if any vandalism was done to my boat! I told him I was serious, and then we laughed. Ivan said that sometimes the men did not know if I was kidding or if I was serious, I told him that it was not important for them to know the difference but only for me to know.

Our goal was to help make the neighborhood unfit for any jap warships so that General MacArthur could make it back to the Philippines as he had promised the millions of Filipinos that had been living under the jap rulers. MacArthur wanted to walk back onto the sands at Leyte Beach, and Nimitz said that we would help him all that we could.

As we kept pushing the japs north, more and more islands would become available for us to use as small garrison bases for the PT boats to hide out at. I had Ivan start getting maps ready of the different islands that were not facing onto the open ocean, and we would have to find some local freighter skipper that really knew the best islands to be able to use.

We would send off a message to Darwin, Australia to see if they could scare up a steamboat captain that wanted to be employed as a "consultant" for the near future. Those are the guys that ran a little steam tramp between the hundreds of islands selling and buying and trading anything they could make a buck with.

These guys knew the islands like the backs of their hands. They would know where a hidden cove would lie so that a couple of PT boats could lay in wait for a jap ship to come along, since they had probably used that cove to hide their smuggled items from the Spanish that ruled the islands for so many years.

We weighed anchor at 21:00, and made our way out of the anchorage, the harbor master that was in charge of putting the ships in lines had done a great job, you had enough room for the ship to swing at anchor and not to hit any other ship. Unless your anchor slipped, then there was all hell to pay. How would you like to be the "Junior-Officer-of-the-Deck" on watch at 03:00 when you have to wake the Admiral up to tell him that his ship had just rear-ended another Admiral's ship? No thank you, keep me in the PT-service, please!

It would take us about three days to hit our new base, some of the other ships with us would drop off at other new bases as we went. I had Ramos pull the staff together for a 06:00 informal breakfast meeting so we could get to know each other a little bit better.

Ramos was my chief of staff, and he had an assistant that was a Lt.(jg), we had a Commander James that was in charge of Communications, and he had a Lt.(jg) as an assistant also. We had a Lieutenant Rogers that was going to be over the PT boat staffing, and we had an Ensign named

Charles, that was a supply expert in real life. In Navy terminology, he was a "Scrounger"!

The scrounger could get you anything you needed, at any time you needed it, and he did not have to put in a request chit through the supply channels and wait for it to be shipped to you, so it arrived six weeks after you needed it. Those kinds of guys were what made the Navy run, with a little grease applied at the right location, you could get your mission done on time, every time.

I used to get things I needed while I was on a PT boat in the Solomon's by trading a box of chocolate bars from home, to a guy that would find me the repair part that we needed for the boat, these scroungers today dealt in new engines for a two and a half ton truck or a rebuilt engine for an airplane and not just for a box of chocolate anymore.

Ivan asked me if I wanted a little shack on the island so that I could relax when I was not working, I said that we would have to see what was available when we got there. He said that maybe a cozy three-bedroom with running water, maybe?

I asked him what he was up to. He said that while I was eating breakfast with the other Admirals on the "Big-E" that he went ashore and found a Seabee Senior Chief that he used to know on Rabaul who still owed him a little favor.

It seems that this Senior-Chief Seabee at Ulithi knew the Senior-Chief of the Seabee Detachment that was on our new island. So, his crew was busy building us a Corrugated Quonset Hut on stilts to keep it dry during the rainy months, and they would build a small wood deck for us to use in the evenings.

When the war was finally over, we could lease it to some local head-hunter tribal chief to live in with his extra wives. Ivan said that the building would be completed within two days, so about the time we pulled in.

They were also busy building a repair depot for PT boats and a longer runway for the fighters and bombers that were assigned to us. Ivan asked me if I saw that big ship on the port bow that had a large crane forward and one aft? I told him that I thought it was just a freighter, he said No Sir, that would be one full-fledged and fully outfitted PT boat Repair Tender that was going to park itself in the bay at a pier that the Seabees were building near the depot.

I asked him what kind of protection did we have for a mother ship of that size and he said that the Seabees were taking care of that also, they were building a special roof that would go over the ship and make it blend into the surrounding natural terrain so that if any enemy bombers happened to come over they would only see part of a mountain that fell off into the bay. They also had a curtain to drape over any PT boat alongside that could not get underway that was camouflaged like the jungle. A lot better than the old-style nets we had used back in '42.

I asked him if there was anything else that I had forgotten? He smiled and said that lunch was ready, a special treat today, toasted Peanut Butter and Jelly sandwiches!

We made landfall about 14:00 at Halamera on the next day, I had forgotten that out here in the war zone you did not work six days and take Sunday off, all the days just ran into one another.

I had asked the ship's Captain earlier at dinner if he could shorten the title that the Boatswain Mate of the watch had to announce over the speaker whenever I came aboard or left the ship? He said that he would come up with something for me, so when I left the ship to check out my beach quarters, they rang me off as "PT-DIVISION-two, DEPARTING!" I smiled and told the Chief of the watch to give my compliments to the Captain.

There was a jeep and a driver on the pier to take Ivan and me to the hut they had built for us. It even had a name plaque and a star on it at the entrance to the steps. The hut was built about three feet above the ground, and there was a wooden veranda of the side that faced the water, wow the Seabees had out-done themselves this time. There were three bedrooms and a bathroom in the center with our own shower. It had hot and cold running water and a small kitchen to boot.

Ivan said that the Seabees would be using a tug-boat to move the Tender into place during the night and by sun-up, we would not even know that there was a ship tied up to the pier. This, I wanted to see so at 02:00 I got up and walked down to the depot area, I did not think about taking my marine guard or asking for a driver to take me but after all the hassle I had getting to the pier I asked for my driver to come and get me when I was finished so that I would not get shot by a trigger-happy sentry on the way back.

Ivan came down with the driver and said that he almost peed his pants laughing when the Sargent of the Guard woke him up asking if he could vouch for some guy that swears, he is the Admiral in charge of this place, but he was not carrying any I.D. on him.

Well, that helped me to remember to always take my marine guard whenever I left my quarters at night.

The Seabees did a wonderful job of covering the top of the ship, and they even painted the wood tops and made it look like a landscape. Ivan was right when he said that from the air you could not even tell there was a repair facility there. Hopefully, this would help if we got caught in an air raid.

I suggested that the Seabees build a fake repair facility on the next bay and to use that old freighter that was run-a-ground out in the channel as a target for any japs to aim at so they would not come looking to close at the real thing in our bay, all they needed was a pier and tow the freighter up to it and rig a fake crane boom over the side. They suggested that we could put some empty box crates over on the pier to make it more convincing. I said make it happen.

Ivan came in the next morning and told me that two out of our PT boats had set up in the Palawan Passage, and had found a destroyer that had run-aground on a shoal and was getting ready to be pulled off by another jap destroyer, they were able to fire two fish at the destroyer that was doing the pulling and sink her, then they were able to sink the stuck destroyer with just one torpedo but most of the sailors were able to swim to shore.

We were going to call in some Army bombers to finish off the destroyer since it was stuck and would not finish sinking. They should be able to hit it since it was not moving. The Army always had a problem hitting a moving target, they would send a dozen bombers after a jap task force and not get a single hit but if the Navy sent in a dozen bombers from a Carrier, they would sink four to five ships of the task group and leave the rest smoking and running for their lives.

I told him that was the kind of news that I liked to hear in the mornings, the butt-kicking kind of news.

He said that other PT boats were going to position themselves around the islands and that we would hit the jap task force that we were told by the "coast-watcher" would be coming back to Borneo to refuel and rearm. They would not be in any position to give a strong chase if their fuel-oil bunkers were low.

I told him that I wished that we had the same kind of Torpedoes that the japs had. The Japanese Long-Lance Torpedo could propel itself almost twenty miles at slow speed, and it carried over a 1000-pound warhead, where-as ours only carried a 600-pound warhead and would only travel about five miles. The japs could sink an aircraft carrier with one shot, but ours would take six or more torpedoes. It was sad that the Naval Ordinance could not bring itself to admit that the enemy had us beaten when it came to Torpedoes.

I told Ivan to make sure that the boats knew to go after the "Tailend-Charlie's," or any damaged ship that could not keep up with the rest of them.

That way the task force commander would only think that the ships ran out of fuel or sank on their own and they would not suspect that we were lying in wait for them. Ramos said that was why I was the boss, I had a devious mind.

Over the next two days, we heard that our boats had picked off another cruiser that was limping back home and that the Submarines in the passage had gotten two destroyers that were a forward guard one day out in front of a two-carrier taskforce that was going to Borneo for fuel.

There was too much heat around a Carrier task force, so I told Commander James to radio all the boats to pull back and let the subs have a few days with them, we would pick them up the next time they sortied.

Lieutenant Rogers said that he had another six boats that were arriving in the next two days and wanted to know where did we want to place them? I told him that Ramos would decide what we needed, so to see him tomorrow, I told Ramos that I really wanted a couple of boats to stay here with us for local protection and that the rest could be sent further up the island chain to set up another forward base.

He said that the Marines had just cleared another island about 100 miles north of us and that the Seabees were busy building an airfield for protection, he would have them set up a Forward Base for four PT boats and crews when they finished the airstrip.

I told him that they would not need that much since they could still use us for a home-base with our tender located here. He agreed that fuel and a few small shacks would suffice for now, as fast as we were moving up, it would not pay to build them a city of their own. Ivan said that he would take care of it all for me.

Over the next week, we worked out a couple of details for an upcoming operation that "ULTRA" brought our way. Apparently, the japs were trying to sucker Halsey and his 3rd fleet into a showdown in the Philippine Sea. Nimitz said that we were not going to allow that to happen, so we needed to step up our game-plan.

I told Ivan that we needed to have more boats out at night to see if we could whittle down the available jap ships, even if we could just damage them to take them out of action would help. We had damaged a few in the past, and they had to send them all the way back to the ship-yards in Japan to get fixed and would be out of circulation for months.

That was what I was talking about with the difference of the torpedoes, a Long Lance could take the whole bow off a cruiser of ours, but our torpedoes would hardly do any damage, so we had to hit them harder with more, to damage or sink them.

I asked Ramos to double the number of boats so that we could do more damage in our areas of responsibility in the next couple of weeks. The only problem was that the japs were not coming out like they used to, so that meant that we would have to go in and find them.

I sent in a request to have some recon-flights over the jap navy bases so that we could see what we were up against in the area, we got the film back with-in twenty-four hours, and it showed us plenty. I asked Ivan if he thought we could slip a couple of boats into a protected harbor during an air raid? He smiled and said sure if they were led by a certain Admiral. I told him that I wished I could but there was no way that would happen anymore, it was time for the younger generation to take the fight to the enemy.

I asked for the earliest possible date that we could get a bomber attack for the jap base at Borneo, either Army or Navy, I did not care.

The Army said that they could send fifty B24s over on Tuesday night and come in from the South and then the Navy said that they had a carrier task-force close enough to send some high-level bombers over on Thursday and come in from the North, but they would have to take off just before dark, and then fly back to an island where they could land safely after dark. It was too dangerous to try to land at night on a ship bouncing around on the high seas so they would fly back on Friday.

This could work out to our benefit, we could catch the japs unaware on Tuesday night and slip in four PT boats and hit them with Torpedoes while they are watching the sky for the bombers attacking and make a clean getaway. Then on Thursday do it all over again, but the bombers come in from a totally different direction, and then the PT boats hit them again during the air attack.

I called a staff meeting for 14:00 today and told everyone the plan. There were no “nay-sayers.” I told James to send off a message to Nimitz telling him that we needed his Carrier on Thursday night and to let General MacArthur know that that we needed the B24s for Tuesday. The show would start at 22:00 on both nights.

I told him to let the PT boats know that they needed to be loaded with good torpedoes and that the show would start when the first bombs started to fall and not before, or it would let the cat out of the bag. They only had a ten-minute window to take their shots and get out before their cover would be blown.

We decided to send in eight boats each night and to have two of them stay at the entrance to the bay just-in-case any patrol craft showed up as a surprise. The perimeter boats would hide at both sides of the entrance to the bay and not join in unless an enemy ship came in and found our PT boats.

I wanted them to do a shoot and scoot and not get caught inside the bay or else the plan for the next bombing would be a bust.

All we had to do now was to wait till Tuesday night at 22:00 and see if we could pull it off without getting caught by the japs. I was a "Nervous Nellie" all day Tuesday, and I started second-guessing myself, praying that if there were any injuries or deaths of my PT-Crews that they would forgive me for sending them into harm's way. This was the part of being a Commanding Officer that I was not used to, and I did not know if I would ever get used to it.

At 21:00 we all gathered in the Combat-Information-Center (C.I.C.) where we could hear all the radio traffic and plot both of our bombers coming and going and also the PT boats as they got underway. Our planes were thirty minutes out and on time and on course. Our PT boats were slipping along the coastline with their mufflers on to hide the sound of those Packard Marine engines.

The only thing that I could not plan for was if the japs had laid any mines in the bay. Hopefully, they did not do it because of the heavy traffic in and out of the bay around the oil-fields. They thought they were safe from our Navy in the bay

The boats were ready to go just before 22:00 and the bombers started dropping their loads right on-time. Our crews did wonderfully, they pulled in during the air raid and let their fish fly. The bombers were instructed to hit the pier area and the ships if possible, in order to keep every eye toward the shore and not toward the bay.

We were able to score four hits with torpedoes on two destroyers and one ammo ship that lit up the sky for miles around, the Army bombers hit two cruisers with their payloads, and they would take months to repair in Japan. Our PT boats got away without being seen so we would have our cryptologists listen in on any radio intercepts over the next day to see what the japs sent off to Tokyo.

We pulled it off, Radio Pearl got an "ULTRA" intercept that the Borneo Navy base had experienced an air-raid by Army land-based, long-range bombers and that there was considerable damage to two cruisers that were going to be escorted back to Japan for repairs.

It was also reported that two destroyers were a total loss and that a 20,000-ton ammo ship was destroyed in the bombing. They were asking for another ammo ship to replace the one lost in the air-attack because the ammo was being sent north to Davao Island to prepare to repel the US Army.

They said that the Cruisers would be escorted by four fast-attack destroyers and they gave the direction of travel and timeline. The only problem was that the cruisers could only pull twelve knots due to damage. Our Submarines would pick them off as they tried to make their way north to Japan.

I had James check on the status of our crews, and they all came out ok, not a scratch, and they got in and out without being seen, which meant that Thursday nights attack was still on. I had Commander James send out a "BRAVO-ZULU" to the PT-crews for a job well-done. They would have a day off to get ready for the next attack, and I wanted the same results as the first one.

I got a message from ComSubPac at Pearl Harbor that they had sent the info out to a couple of subs in the South China Sea, to try to intercept the cruisers that were en route to the shipyards in Japan, he hoped that they would be able to finish them off before they got home.

I found out that the Army had landed at Davao in the Southern Philippines, they were going to have a tough fight ahead of themselves, yes, there were hundreds of islands, but there were only like tend major islands that they would defend to the death.

Ivan said that we were busy making another advance base up the chain of islands, this would save our boats over 200 miles one way for refit and replenishment of torpedoes and supplies. I told him to check with the Army to see when they would mark the area as secure so that we might move the

Mount McKinley up into Philippine waters. It looked like it was time to hang a "For Lease" sign on my hut.

The PT boats went out again at the same time on Thursday night, and the Carrier had launched the Navy Bombers at 19:00, it should take them just under three hours flying time to get to the Navy base at Borneo. I hoped that they did not run into any headwinds that would throw the time-table off.

Commander James sent a message to the PT-Squadron to wait for the bombs to fall just-in-case the bombers were late, I hoped that they were on-time, but you had to plan for the unexpected.

On the radio net, we heard the bombers say that they were going to start their runs in 10-minutes, that meant that they were already fifteen minutes late so what was this going to do to our PT boat schedule. Hopefully, they would be smart enough to wait through the delay.

Commander James's assistant came into the C.I.C. and said that they had picked up radio traffic that the PT boats had ran into some problem out in the entrance of the bay, we were still trying to make sense of it. Apparently, they had just gotten intercepted by two fast patrol craft, and they were taking fire. I asked Ramos if there were any fighter cover for the bombers? He said that he did not know, but that he doubted it, due to the distance from the ship.

The PT boats had been discovered before they could get into the bay, now we were waiting on the bombers to provide a distraction to see if they could get out of there, we did not know if they could still fire the torpedoes or not. The bombers started their runs, and they got some hits, so we were trying to contact the PT boats to pull the plug on the rest of the mission.

I had James send out the "Abort-Code" to all units involved. This was not how it was supposed to go down, it was supposed to be a simple shoot and scoot, a simple cake-walk! Ramos took my arm and led me off to the side. He reminded me that rule#1 was that good guys were going to die in war-time, and rule#2 was that no matter what bosses did, they could NOT change rule#1.

I told James to rescind the abort order and tell them to "KILL JAPS" and more JAPS, finish the job they were sent to do!

The PT boats moved in for a second try at the ships moored at the piers, they fought it out with the fast-patrol craft and traded them one for one. They blasted one of our boats right out of the water with a five-inch gun mounted on their bow, but we were able to shoot a torpedo that the second boat turned right into, he sunk within thirty seconds after a horrendous explosion. The first enemy craft ran into the bay after the rest of the PT boats, the bombers were just finishing up with their bomb runs. At least three ships were on fire at the refueling piers, and one of the fuel terminals was blazing away. Our boats sent off a couple of torpedoes to see if they could finish off the damaged ships and then they made a run for it.

Two of our boats took damage during the runout, and some of the Navy bombers took Anti-Aircraft damage, maybe we had stretched our luck a little too far. It looked like the japs tonight were ready for another repeat of Tuesday night, only this time, they did not want to get caught with their pants down, or their hand in the Saki jar.

The radio was blaring reports of a couple of the boats that needed medical care for wounded men. The Navy bombers were within sixty minutes of reaching the alternate air-strip, and then we would find out how they came out. It sounded like I was going to have to write some of those dreaded letters home to loved ones again.

I had fourteen dead, and six wounded out of the eight different boats, and the Navy bombers had lost four planes in the drink on the way back to the airstrip.

They had one plane crash on landing killing both of the crewmen, so that was ten aviators and fourteen PT-sailors dead for a half-baked idea to sink some jap ships. The next morning Ivan had a message from Admiral Nimitz telling me that my operation was a success and that the japs were pulling more assets to try to protect the oil-fields on Borneo, this would take more of them away from bases around the Philippine Islands, and he said that was a good thing!

He also told me to dispatch some of my resources up north of our new island hideaway, and maybe they could catch some of the troop transports out at sea and sink them before they could get to Borneo. I told Ramos to make it happen.

I asked Ivan if the Seabees were going to make us another hut at each island, he laughed and said he doubted it. He said maybe the Scrounger could come up with something to make our life easier when we get to the new base. He had not been doing much lately for us.

I got the information on the dead and wounded and set down that night to write some short letters, I explained in each of the letters that their loved ones did not die in vain, they died doing what they loved, and for what they believed in. I asked them not to discuss the situations they were involved with due to national security and signed them as Admiral James Beck-USNR, Commander-Motor Torpedo Boat Division #2. Ramos thought that was a nice touch, he said that most Admirals would never bother writing a letter for all the men lost under their command.

I told him that we were both there at one time, and I kind of knew how the family would feel. My mom never got a letter explaining how my brother had died off of Tulagi that night. Maybe she would have excepted it easier if a letter had come.

I got a "Well Done" message from both Admiral Halsey and Admiral Nimitz on the Borneo Operation, they said that between the bombers and our PT boats, we were responsible for taking out two Heavy Cruisers, one Light Cruiser, and six Destroyers. Both Heavy Cruisers were sunk by submarines on their way to the Japan shipyards for repairs in the last week, and the oil terminal that was blown up in Borneo was still blazing away. Our guys did a great job again.

We made plans to move north the next week, I was going to miss the hut that I had on the beach, I bet Ivan that some headhunter chief was going to enjoy it after we left. He just smiled!

There was a group of fifteen islands that had a large channel running between them that the Army had cleared west of Davao, it was about 250-miles north of us, and by having a dozen smaller islands out-board of our island, we would be hidden from view by any passing ships. They had a nice beach that the Navy Seabees were building two large piers against it and another repair shop for the PT boats.

They decided not to build the camo roof for the tender to hide under, they did not think it was needed since we had the japs on the run.

The next day we got our first reports on what they were already calling "The Great Marianna's Turkey Shoot." The japs had sortied their fleet to try to protect the Marianna group of islands.

I guess that Admiral Marc (Pete) Mitscher, had set up a trap by using another Carrier Task Force as bait to get the jap navy to commit five Fast Carriers and four light Carriers with over 750 front-line pilots from the jap carriers and also from island bases close to the battle to go after the bait, but in reality there was another US Navy Carrier Task Force with seven Fast Fleet carriers and eight Escort Carriers loaded with backup aircraft onboard them if they were needed.

The backups were not needed. The radio traffic had our pilots saying that it was like shooting fish in a barrel, the japs kept sending more pilots out, and we kept shooting them down as fast as they came at them. Over the next week, we would also bomb their carriers and sink three of them. Our submarine USS Albacore sent fish into the side of INJ Carrier Taiho and then the submarine USS

Cavalla sent her fish into the belly of the INJ Carrier Shokaku.

Both carriers stayed afloat after the torpedo attacks, until the fuel vapors from millions of gallons of leaking aviation gasoline was sent into the ventilation systems by an inexperienced, but well-meaning, Damage Control Officer, sent a fire-ball over 1000-feet into the air, dooming both carriers into the deep abyss of the Marianna Trench which is over 36,000 feet deep.

When the carriers sunk into the deep waters of the Pacific Ocean, they both took over 1200 sailors and pilots that manned the 90 airplanes on-board, into the deep with them.

Our PT-Division had not even set up in a new base of operations when the Army would notify me that they had secured another island area for us. We were going to move again. I told Ramos to tell the boat crews that they needed to plan on living on their boats until we got to an area that we could call our own.

The Army started using our boats as a delivery service to drop off men and materials behind enemy lines, we could circle around and come in on a deserted section of the island and drop the men off and get out of the area before the japs knew that we had even been there.

General MacArthur made his famous return to the Philippines at Leyte Gulf, and our boats were there to provide him some protection, we were on our way to Tokyo Bay, and there was no stopping us now.

Admiral Halsey returned to the Central Pacific in command of Third Fleet, and he was barreling toward Tokyo, the islands in the Pacific Ocean were too far apart, so that left the PT boats in the back of any plans that were made. We were busy all around the Philippines doing what we did best so we would leave the big islands of the Pacific to Halsey and his boys.

Everyone that I knew thought that President Roosevelt would guide us all the way to our final victory in this two-ocean war that we did not want.

On April 12,1945 we were notified in a message to all troops that he had died, there was total silence on the ship. Nobody knew anything about this guy Harry S. Truman that was the vice-president, he was always in the shadows whenever the President was in the news.

We did not know if he had what it would take to push the japs all the way back to Tokyo or would he allow them to sue for peace? We got a message from Nimitz that everything we had planned was still a go and that we could best Honor President Roosevelt by working our way into Tokyo Bay and winning the war like he had wanted.

We had boats spread all around the islands, and they were giving us a good show for the money, they were harassing the japs whenever they found them.

The Army was making a big landing in Leyte Gulf, and we were going to send some boats around the west side of the Philippines because "ULTRA" had said that the japs were going to try to upset General MacArthur's plan for a landing by sending two different task groups by sea. One would come in from the San Bernardino Strait, and the other would come by way of the Surigao Strait just north of Mindanao.

The central force ran into a couple of our submarines while they were out to sea and they were able to damage a few of the ships. The central force turned around and acted like they were going to leave but then reversed course and continued on towards Leyte Gulf. We did not have any PTs in the area at that time.

We set a trap for the southern force using twelve PT boats while the jap ships were in the confines of the straight, we were able to hit four ships with torpedoes, two sank right away, and the other two had to turn around. This caused the other jap ships to become confused, with the fog and the smoke of the battle making it difficult to see what was really happening at first, they also turned around but changed their minds later and continued up the straight into the trap laid in by our Battleships.

We had seven old battleships that were waiting at the head of the straight and were ready to "Cross the Enemies-T" this was a way to bring every heavy gun to bare and be able to fire at the same time at the enemy that could only fire to forward or chance hitting their own ships.

We devastated the enemy line of battle in the south, but we had only damaged the central fleet, and they were bearing down on the small carrier task force (Taffy-3) that was setting off the beach at Leyte Gulf.

Our carrier planes were set up with fragmentation bombs used for protection of the troops ashore, not with bombs made to penetrate ships. We were soon to find out what the sailor's term for the CVE (combustible-very-expendable) really meant. The first we knew that the japs were coming was when sixteen-inch shells started falling among the carriers. The carriers were doing fourteen knots launching and landing planes, but now they had to try to evade the incoming jap shells so the planes could not land.

Admiral Kinkade sent his destroyers after the japs, I wish that we would have had some PT boats in the area to help, but we did not. We were told that the japs had turned around and sailed back to Japan, but they had changed course in the night and were now after our fleet.

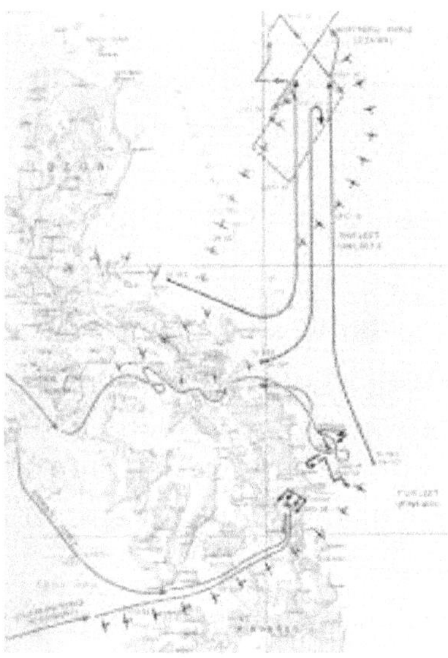

#32 Map courtesy of Wikipedia

Admiral Halsey was off chasing the jap northern fleet, he was told to protect the Army at Leyte Gulf, but then he was also told to sink the jap fleet if he had a chance. He saw the opportunity to go after the fleet, and he did.

Admiral Kinkade sent off a message to Third Fleet asking for help immediately, and the jap admiral was afraid that the US Battleships would be coming over the horizon, so they pulled out and turned back toward Japan. Our aircraft pursued the jap fleet and sunk one of the largest battleships ever made, the Musashi, a sister ship to the mighty Yamato weighing in at 70,000 tons and measuring a whopping 865 feet long and 128 feet across at its widest point, she carried 2800 men, and they were all lost at sea.

We lost many ships and sailors during those battles over a couple of days, but we still got the win overall. The Yamato was damaged in the early stages of the battle and fled to Kure Naval yard in Japan for repairs.

For security Admiral Halsey had me send twelve PT boats to a base close to Leyte to help protect all the navy ships that were off-loading men and equipment onto the beaches. We were changing from an attacking force to a security force. I even moved my command ship into the area to be able to be closer to the front lines.

Chapter 17 - From Okinawa to the Bomb

The Marines invaded Okinawa, and after a tough eighty-two-day battle they finally took the island, the japs lost 110,000 soldiers and sailors, and the US lost over 12,500 soldiers killed on the island and almost 7,500 sailors killed on the navy ships that were targets of the Kamikaze air attacks. The navy lost twenty-four ships sunk and another 386 damaged, the air-attacks went around the clock without a let-up for days on end.

The jap super-battleship Yamato was sunk by a combination of our submarines and our aircraft from Admiral Halsey's carriers. It was being sent to defend the Okinawa Island and was caught in the open sea. All 3000 sailors were lost with the ship.

This one ship boasted 18. One-inch main battle guns that could fire a 3000-pound shell almost twenty-six miles. If it had been turned loose at the beginning of the war, we would not be in the place that we were at now.

With the end of the Japanese battle fleets as we knew them, it was basically just a cleanup job now around the islands, the japs were trying to get away by using barges again. Now, we had a really good radar to help find them, just like we learned to use back in Melville.

We had air-superiority through-out the islands, and we could call in air support whenever we needed help, and that was almost every day.

I asked for a liaison to start working alongside us so that we could get a quicker response when aircraft are called in for support. They sent us a Commander Lee, he was an aviator and had spent a few years flying fighter aircraft from carriers. He was single, and Admiral Halsey knew him personally.

I had heard that Commander Lee was dating the Admiral's granddaughter, Cassondra, and they planned on getting married when the war was over. I guess the Admiral wanted to make sure he would have great-grandkids when he retired.

So, what better way, but to transfer your future grandson-in-law to a safe desk away from the flight-line.

I told Lee when he came aboard that he would be working with my Commander James from radio comms. I let him know that we needed to keep our ready board updated so that when I needed a squadron of fighters, I would know where they were located and how long it would take them to respond to our calls. I also wanted to have some bombers on a thirty-minute alert just-in-case we found any stray enemy ships that we could not get a PT boat quick enough.

His answer was a resounding "Can-Do Sir!" He might fit in here ok. Now if I could only get Ramos trained like that.

We were able to try this out a week later when we had some Pt's out barge hunting, and they came upon a fleet of twelve armored barges trying to slip between some islands. We only had two boats against twelve barges, and they were not only armored, but they were well armed also. Our boats called for help, and Lee found a squadron of Corsairs that had come in a few hours earlier and were refueled and rearmed and just sitting at an airfield about thirty minutes away. They got airborne, and our PT boats pulled away to make the japs think that they had a free pass, with Lee on the radio to the aircraft and James on the radio to our boats, we left nothing alive or afloat on the water when we were done.

Each of those barges had to carry around 100 men, and the ones that we did not kill with our guns were attacked and killed by the sharks in the waters around those Philippine islands. We used to see large groups of sharks all around the islands, you did not want to fall overboard, especially if you were wounded and bleeding. One small drop of blood in the water was like a radar to a shark, and he always called for help from other sharks.

At least getting killed by a shark would be rather quick, how would you like to fall overboard in the Banda Sea east of Celebes, there we found schools of millions of poisonous green water-snakes just floating on the waves, sunning themselves. It actually looked like a large piece of carpet, only it was moving and writhing around. I had never seen anything like that before, and I hoped that I would never see it again.

I was still in charge of all the PT boats assigned to the Philippine waters, we had added more staff members to help carry the war to Japan's backdoor. Our ship was roughly, twice as big as the ship that Halsey had used in the Solomon Islands, and we needed every room. There were some of the younger officers that had to use a broom closet as an office, well it worked. As long as they could sit at a small desk and have a chair, they could call it their "office."

Some of the boats in the south were starting to complain that the only thing they ever saw while out on patrol, was another PT boat, so we decided to move more of them, north.

With the completion of the air-bases at Okinawa and on Saipan and Tinian in the Marianas, we were able to start bombing Japan itself. Our B-52 bombers could fly the whole mission and return, even though it would be an eleven-hour trip, it was done. We did not have any fighters that could go the distance, so we always had to station submarines and even PT boats on lifeguard duty at pre-arraigned locations in-case they had to ditch in the ocean because of battle damage.

Our boats would monitor a special radio frequency that the bombers would come up on if they needed help. We would identify them and tell them where we were located so they could try to fly closer to us. Our maps were cut into sections, and you would tell the pilot that we were in map section George-75 and he would fly that direction. There were some boats that even got the airplane water ditching crash on home movies, then moved in for the rescue. We were able to save a lot of airmen that way.

One month later we were told that a special bomb had been dropped on Japan, that it was so big, that it wiped out a whole city named Hiroshima. Then six days later another bomb was dropped on Nagasaki. We could not comprehend the notion of a single bomb wiping out a whole city and killing 80,000 people in one blast but, better them, then us.

We were notified the next day that Japan had agreed to our surrender terms, the crew was yelling and screaming and pounding each other on their backs.

Admiral Halsey sent out a message for us to be ready to take any japs prisoner if they came forward with a white flag but to be ready for any tricks, and not to let our guard down one bit. I let my boat commanders know that they should approach any jap sub or ship with extreme caution and be ready to fire at all times, if something looked wrong shoot first, and ask questions later. I would stand up for any member of my squadron.

Admiral Halsey sent me a message that he wanted twenty-four of my PT boats to help escort them into Tokyo bay to get ready for the actual signing of the “instrument of surrender.” It would take place on the USS Missouri BB-61; this ship was named after President Truman’s home state of Missouri.

We had a jap cruiser, and two damaged jap destroyers lead the way into the bay just in-case there were any mines that had been laid to catch our ships. We sent in four minesweepers and the PT boats to search the bay before the Missouri went in. Our men stood at the ready with machine guns and carbines until we knew that the japs were serious about the surrender.

Our air support kept reporting to us that they were finding US soldiers standing up on the roofs of their barracks in P.O.W. camps, so we sent in Marines to liberate them. We had some landing craft, and PT boats go right up to the shoreline and take men onboard, they took them back out to troop ships until we could get a hospital ship into the harbor.

We never found any of the camp commanders or camp guards at the P.O.W. camps, they had fled in civilian clothes before we got there. That was probably smart on their part because I know what I felt when I saw what our soldiers looked like and I heard the stories these guys were telling us.

I could not blame anyone for shooting a sadistic guard that had beaten these men repeatedly for nothing that he ever did. We had to reign in our feelings and keep our men on a short lease.

We got the Hospital ship USS Comfort (AH-6) in-port, and they were busy loading ex-prisoners on-board so they could take them to Guam and return for more. From Guam, they would be flown back to Pearl or kept in the hospital until they could travel on a troop ship or another hospital ship depending on if they needed medical care or not.

#33 US Navy Photo Courtesy of Wikipedia

Some of these hospital ships were manned by Navy medical corps and some by Army medical corps. They had Navy personnel manning the ship but army doctors to provide care for the injured. My PT boats provided security for these ships when they came in to pick up our men.

I received a message that I needed to report to the Hospital ship at Pier #15 the next morning. Apparently, they had found a couple of PT-sailors among the P.O.W prisoners in one of the camps that were just liberated. They wanted to check them out and start them on medicine and fluids before they could talk to anyone. I told Ivan that I wanted him to go with me along with a marine guard at 09:00 the next day.

Ivan had a Marine Sgt. armed with a Thompson standing by at 08:30. We had a landing craft take us from the ship to the personnel landing where another Marine was waiting with a jeep, he drove us to the Hospital ship. They were busy loading ex-prisoners unto the ship, some were walking, and some were on litters being carried aboard. They all looked terrible, their skin was shrunken to their bones, and they were all malnourished, and their clothes were in tatters.

I checked in with the Officer of the Deck and was told that the PT-Sailors were on the 3rd deck. We made our way down to the third deck and checked in with the duty nurse at the desk. She said that there were fifteen PT-Sailors that I could speak to, there were a few that were in such bad shape that they might not make it back to Guam.

We made our way down the passageway into a berthing area and started interviewing each man. We asked their names and serial numbers first, then we asked them what PT boat they were assigned to? Some of these guys had been prisoners for up to almost four years, and they looked like it. Ivan was talking to this one guy that was skin and bones, and he said, "Admiral, you might want to hear this one."

I walked over and stood over his shoulder as the sailor was starting to answer the questions. His voice was really hoarse and raspy, but I could still hear his answers. He said that he was lost off of Tulagi Island in the Solomon Islands back in December 1942. His boat had been cut in half by a jap destroyer, and the rest of the crew was lost in the explosion.

This guy had floated on a piece of wood for two days when he was picked up by a jap submarine. He was taken to an island and put on a freighter and sent to first Rabaul then on to the Philippines and then finally to Japan. He had been beaten at every opportunity, they had even pulled his teeth out with plyers with-out any anesthesia or painkillers. He told them when they captured him that he was a new ensign that had fallen overboard from a cruiser in order to hide the fact that he was a PT boat skipper.

Something was familiar about this guy, I asked Ivan what boat he was on. He said it was PT-66 and that he was with Squadron #2 out of Tulagi. I could not believe what I was hearing, could it be? I looked closely at him, and then I said, "Mike, is that you?"

He stopped talking and looked at me. He said, "Yes sir, my name is Mike Beck, I was the skipper on PT-66."

I almost started crying, was this really my brother? This guy looked like he weighed in at eighty pounds wet and he looked to be eighty years old! I leaned over to Ivan and told him to write down all his information so we could verify it first. Ivan looked at me kind of funny, so I told him just do it, and I will explain in a little bit.

When we walked out of earshot of the sailors, I told Ivan that the Ensign he was talking to might be my brother. I wanted to talk to the Doctor to see what kind of condition he was in and what the prognosis was for him. I found the Doctor, and he looked up his chart, he said that it was going to be a long haul for the guy, they had him on a strict diet due to the malnourishment, and they were treating him for Beri-Beri and Scurvy. He also had two broken bones that did not heal properly, but the doctors at Pearl would decide if they would do surgery to repair that or not.

I asked the doctor if he was going to make it or not, he said that was up to the patient and God, not him. He said that if the patient had something to live for, that it would improve his chances a lot. I decided that I was going to give him something to live for.

I sent the Sgt. with us back to the ship to get a picture of my folks from my office desk, I told Ivan that I wanted him to verify the serial number and the dates of the sailor before I met with him. He said that it could take up to two hours, but he would go to the radio room and send off a flash message to Pearl. Ramos got the reply in a little over two hours, and he had the dates and serial number of my brother to check against what the P.O.W. had told him.

Ivan found me in the wardroom getting a sandwich and a cup of coffee, he said, looks like you have a brother again Admiral!

We ate while we waited for the Sgt. to come with the photograph. As soon as he came, we were ready to go see this guy again. He was asleep when we got to his rack, they had him on a couple of I.V.s to give him fluids and some meds that his system needed before he could be started on any solid foods.

I sat in a chair beside him and took a breath. I laid my hand on his arm and spoke softly to him, I did not want to startle him awake after what he had been through. He looked up at me and said, “Sir, was there something else you needed?”

I asked him if he could look at a picture that I had, and identify the man and woman in it? He said he would try. He took one look and teared up right away. He said, “That looks like my mom and dad, where did you get that at?” I smiled and said, “Are you sure? I happen to know this couple pretty good and that I am not sure if they would accept you as one of their three boys.” He looked at me, and that little smirk came across his face as it finally started to register with him.

He wanted to know just how far I had to chase this Admiral to steal his uniform or did I find it in the cleaners and just on a whim decided to borrow it for a while? I laughed and told him that I had earned each and every stripe on this uniform and that Admiral Nimitz would vouch for me. He wanted to know if it was really over? I told him yes, we had beat them back to Japan and that the

Surrender ceremony was to be held in a couple of days right here in Tokyo Bay.

We found out that the ship would be getting under-way in the morning around 06:00 to make way for another hospital ship. This one would be full by then, and they wanted to get them back to Pearl Harbor.

I told Mike that I would send the folks a message telling them about him being alive and that I would probably meet up with him at Pearl since he was going to be there a while to recover. I told him that he needed to take it easy and keep his head up, it would be a long road but that I wanted to keep him around for a little while yet so that we could do some of those plans we had made before the war.

He said that sounded like a good plan to him. He said, "How are you going to find me at Pearl?" I said, "Hey, brother, I found you once I can find you again."

I was told in a message from Admiral Halsey that he wanted me to be onboard the USS Missouri by 06:00 the next morning to be a witness of the surrender. He said to make sure I was early because there was going to be many dignitaries on the ship, he was sending over a ships-pass for Ramos and myself. They would have our name on the guest list and take us to the spot we would stay at for the ceremony.

I got ahold of Ivan and told him to get our best uniforms cleaned and pressed and told him what we were going to do in the morning. He almost fell out of his chair when I finished reading him the message from "Bull" Halsey. He could not believe it, he was going to be able to see the final surrender of Japan.

We had come so far, and it had taken a lifetime for some of our people, we could not have done it without the men that gave their lives on hundreds of small islands and over thousands of sea miles. It was sobering to think of all the lives that had been lost since December 7th, 1941. I had made it to the end.

We went to the official ceremony and had ringside standing positions on the main deck so we could see and hear without the sound system.

#34 US Navy Photo Courtesy of Wikipedia

It took us two hours to get off the ship. It was a good thing that Ivan brought along some peanut butter and jelly sandwiches for us because we had last eaten breakfast at 03:30, we left for the battleship at 05:00 and had to wait in line for all the official boats and gigs to make their way alongside and deposit their riders. There was so much brass on-board that ship that I am surprised that it did not tip over.

Halsey sent a message to me that he would come by the Mt. Whitney when he left the Missouri to speak to me. I got back to our ship and told the Captain that Halsey was going to stop by so to have enough side-boys available to render a proper salute. He sent the ship into a general cleaning quarters to get it swept down and mopped.

Admiral Halsey got there about three hours later, and we went to my quarters to speak. He told me to start getting my list of boats and personal together, they were going to start the downsizing within thirty days. It would start with the men that had the most points, and we would shift the other men that were left to man other boats. As a boat lost its crew, we were told to beach all the boats on the beach and to burn them.

The navy in its infinite wisdom said that it would cost too much money to ship those boats home, and they did not want them falling into the wrong hands. I told him maybe we should sell them to the locals, and he said negative, we would burn them and list them for the navy to remove from the naval registry.

I wished that I could take one home with me when I leave, I would love to run it up and down the Lake Michigan coastline. But I would have to get my old crew together to make it run, and that was not going to happen.

Ramos could not believe that we were just going to burn our boats on some beach, but I assured him that was the plan, and that ours is not to question why but to do or die. He said, "Aye-Aye Sir!" and he walked out shaking his head.

We took our command ship back to the Philippines to our last base since it was close to Clark Airfield and Subic Bay Naval Station, I figured that the men could fly out of there.

I got my lists together, and we waited until we were notified that they were going to start processing out the men with enough time in service. We had them come up to us as they were notified so that I could personally shake their hands and thank them for a job well done.

It was going nice until I had to greet over 100 men in a single day, I swear that I did not get anything else done that day. Ramos just laughed when I complained to him about it.

He suggested that I have them assemble in a hanger on base and I could meet them there and walk down the ranks if I wanted to still make it personal. We could do it every other day to simplify things and then they could get their travel orders and make their way back home again. If they had to fly out early, that was their choice, but I still wanted to thank them if possible.

I got to see some of the men that I had in school at Melville, they looked a lot older now than when we went through the classes, I guess that we all had aged some over the last four years. For some of the men, it was like an old high school reunion, for others it was difficult to take the news of an old friend that did not make it to the end of the war with them.

There was two Commanders that I had gone to school within Melville that could not believe that Admiral James Beck, was, in fact, the same Ensign Beck that had shared a barracks with in October of

1942! I invited them to go to dinner with me when we were finished up here so that we could get caught up over a couple of drinks before they left for home. After we separated, I might never see these men again, so I wanted this to be special since we had started this war together and now, we were going to finish it together. We had a good time talking about all the men we had worked with since we had started.

We exchanged home addresses so that we could try to keep in touch after we got home, one of them lived in Indianapolis, Indiana and attended Notre Dame also and I told him that we could get together some time for an alumni football game. The second man was from Boston and had attended Harvard, he had almost lost his "Boston accent." I told him he would never fit in around Boston anymore. He said, "watch me." Then we said our good-byes, and they left the war behind.

Ramos's name came up on the rotation list, but he said that he wanted to see this thing through to the end with me, he said that he saw my name also, but that Flag personal did not count so he would feel out of place without me keeping him on the straight and narrow. I thanked him for being along for the ride.

At the start of the war we had thirteen boats in the Subic Bay area when I got to Guadalcanal, we had about fifty boats in all the Pacific Ocean. When Division-2 started moving up around the Philippines, we had over 1000-PT boats at our disposal, now we were down to 250, and that was shrinking every day.

On the first of the month, I was notified that I would be leaving on the 30th, and be going home, my time was up in this war. I was going to miss that throaty roar of the PT boats that I fell in love with at the Navy Yard so long ago. I was going to miss all these good men that I had gone through so much with.

On the 15th. I received a personal letter from Admiral Halsey telling me how he could not have gotten to Tokyo Bay without my help, he said that my team worked so many long hours and that he appreciated it very much. He also said that he was putting both Ramos and I, in for the Distinguished Service Cross and a few others. He knew that General MacArthur was also putting us in for a Meritorious Service Award from the Army for services rendered during the long climb back to the Philippine Islands.

He told me to stop in at Pearl Harbor to say good-bye to him and Admiral Nimitz on my way to the states, they would have a medal ceremony and a small dinner for us.

I told Ivan to be ready to leave by the 29th. He said that he was already packed and could not wait to get home to Chelsea again and get on with his life. I asked him what he wanted to do when he got home, he said that he thought about going back to school and getting a teaching degree. He said that it was fun teaching at Melville and that he might like it.

I told him that I was not sure what I wanted to do yet, maybe teaching was something to look into. I could not really see myself working at a factory after what I had done during the war. Also, there were thousands of men going home to work in the factories again, and the workforce was swelling every day. Jobs were going to be scarce again, just like in the depression.

We said our good-byes to our staff and turned everything over to a new team to finish up the de-mobilization of the American Navy PT boats left here in the islands. I asked the "scrounger" if he could send a complete PT boat to me for Christmas, he said to watch my stocking.

On the flight back to Pearl Harbor I asked Ivan what he was going to miss the most? He said that he would miss the mid-night rides in the Solomon's looking for japs. I agreed with him on that point and then told him that last of all, I was going to miss those blasted peanut butter and jelly sandwiches for breakfast, lunch, and dinner!

The End

Photo and Map Credits

#1-US Navy Photo MTB Base Melville, R.I.-Wikipedia

#2- Photo by Wikipedia- Elco Boat Co-1942-Wikipedia

#3- Elco PT Boat Diagram,1944- Wikipedia

#4- US Navy Photo, author unknown, Wikipedia 1944

#5- photo by Australian War Museum, Wikipedia 1943

#6- photo by Australian War Museum, Wikipedia 1943

#7- US Navy Photo-1942 Wikipedia

#8- Panama Canal Map, Wikipedia 1943

#8A- Canal Cert by Author

#9- US Navy Polly-Wog ceremony by Author

#9A Photo by Author

#10- Photo by Author

#10A- Photo by Author

#10B- Photo by Author

#11- Photo by Author

#12- Photo by Author

#13- Photo by Author

#14- Map of the Solomon Islands by Wikipedia

#15- US Navy Photo making pancakes by PT Museum

#16- US Navy Map, courtesy of US Navy PT boat Museum

#17- US Navy Photo of "Duck" by FlickR.com (Wikipedia)

#18- PT-170 Camouflage by NAVSOURCE Wikipedia

#19- US Navy PT-Tender BY NAVSOURCE Wikipedia

#20- Marston Mats by Sea-bee Museum, Wikipedia

#21- US Navy build a run-way by Sea-bee museum

#22- Photo by US Navy National Seabee Museum

#23- Drawing by Elco Boat Co. Wikipedia

#24- Map up the Guinea Bird US Army- Wikipedia

#25- US Navy Photo- Makalapa 1944 Wikipedia

#26- US Navy Photo- Adm. Nimitz Wikipedia

#27- Black-Cat Photo by MWM-AU, Wikipedia

#28- US Navy Photo 40 mm Bo-for Wikipedia

#29- US Navy Photo Ulithi Atoll- Wikipedia

#30- US Navy Photo Floating Dry-Dock- Public Domain

#31- Map of Southern Philippine Islands Wikipedia

#32- Drawing of Marianna Trench by Wikipedia

#33- US Navy Hospital Ship Photo by Wikipedia

#34- Final Japanese Surender US Navy Photo Wikipedia

Printed in Great Britain
by Amazon

80347547R00130